Praise for
An Elderly Lady Is Up to No Good

"This elderly lady stops at nothing in her
desire for a peaceful existence. I ought to
feel guilty for enjoying her crimes, but I
don't. The stories are written with such
persuasive logic and delicious irony that I
want the killing to continue indefinitely."

—Peter Lovesey, Mystery Writers
of America Grand Master

"A juicy dose of senior justice.
The book is pure fun."

—*Kirkus Reviews*

AN
ELDERLY
LADY
IS UP TO
NO GOOD

ALSO BY HELENE TURSTEN

The Irene Huss Investigations

The Embla Nyström Investigations

AN ELDERLY LADY IS UP TO NO GOOD

HELENE TURSTEN

TRANSLATED BY MARLAINE DELARGY

SOHO CRIME

First English translation published in 2018 by
Soho Press
853 Broadway
New York, NY 10003

Library of Congress Cataloging-in-Publication Data
is available upon request.

ISBN 978-1-64129-011-1
eISBN 978-1-64129-012-8

Printed in the United States of America

10 9 8 7 6 5 4

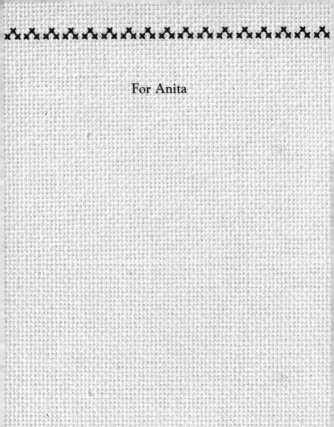

For Anita

TABLE OF CONTENTS

T HE SHRILL SOUND of the doorbell sliced through the silence. Maud sat motionless in her armchair, making no attempt to get up. She knew the bell would soon ring again. And again. And again. This had been going on for weeks.

The reason behind the whole thing was her living arrangements, which were rather unusual.

The apartment in which Maud lived was the only thing her family had managed to hold on to after her father's sudden death from a heart attack. Until then he had kept up appearances, but when he died the family lawyer quickly discovered there was virtually no money left. The only thing of value was the large apartment building in the Vasastan district of Gothenburg. When it was sold, the lawyer managed to work out an agreement with the new owner.

To put it briefly, a clause was inserted in the contract stating that the widow and her two daughters should be allowed to remain in their apartment without paying any rent; they simply had to cover the cost of electricity, water, and heating. In return, the buyer was given the opportunity to purchase the building at a very reasonable price. In addition, the clause stated that "for as long as any member of the family wishes to reside in the apartment, no rent will be payable." A few lines further down it was made clear that the term "member of the family" referred only to the widow and her two daughters. Seventy years had passed since the contract had been drawn up, and at the time no one could have envisaged that one of the daughters would still be living there.

Of course there had been a dispute over the interpretation of the original contract when the building was taken over by a housing association many years later, but after taking the matter to court, Maud won the day, and still lived rent-free. The members of the housing association board ground their teeth in frustration, but there was nothing they could do, though they did win a small victory when it was established that Maud had to pay a small monthly sum toward the general maintenance of the apartment building.

It had now been about forty years since Maud's sister died, leaving her with no living relatives. Maud lived alone, and she went on vacation alone. That was the way she wanted it. Freedom, no idle chatter, and no problems. Idle chatter and problems were the worst things she could think of, and now she was faced with one of the biggest problems she had ever encountered. And she just couldn't see a way out.

MAUD REALIZED SHE had only herself to blame. She had walked straight into the trap with her eyes wide open. Even though a little voice inside her head had tried to warn her, she could never have imagined how badly things would turn out! It had all begun so innocently.

5

During the spring, a genuine celebrity had moved into the building—a woman who was about forty years old, by the name of Jasmin Schimmerhof. She was famous mainly because her parents were famous. As the only child of two of Sweden's best-known personalities, she experienced the trauma of growing up with parents who were totally preoccupied with their respective careers. Neither of them had much time to spare for their daughter, if any. A series of nannies and boarding schools were responsible for Jasmin's upbringing. Her father was a successful financier, and her mother had been one of the country's most internationally renowned opera singers. She toured the great opera houses of the world and was rarely at home with her husband and daughter. Jasmin's mother had died in a car accident just outside New York a few years earlier. Nobody knew how it had happened because she had been alone when she crashed into a concrete column supporting an overpass. The newspapers showed pictures of the grieving widower, but there was no sign of Jasmin. After a period of intense undercover work by tabloid journalists, it emerged that she had been admitted to a private rehab clinic; she had been abusing both legal and illegal drugs, as well as drinking heavily. Her condition was so unstable that she wasn't even able to attend her mother's funeral. The trigger for the abuse was rumored to be her divorce from husband number two six months earlier. Both her first and second marriages had been childless. The press got plenty of headlines out of the tragedy, reveling in the misery of such a powerful family. Media interest flared up again when Ian Schimmerhof, Jasmin's father, got married again six months later—to a woman forty years his junior. From the paparazzi shots taken at the couple's wedding in Switzerland, where they were now living, it was very clear that the new wife was heavily pregnant. A month or so later, Jasmin gained a half-sibling forty years younger than her. The headline writers had a field day, speculating on whether Maria Schimmerhof's car crash really had been an accident—or suicide.

Over the next two years, no one had heard

much about Jasmin Schimmerhof. It was said she was writing her autobiography, and when the book was published, it became an instant bestseller; everyone wanted to know what life had really been like behind the stylish façade of the enormous villa in Örgryte. A number of reviews may have hinted that the use of language was poor, the descriptions of the characters somewhat flat, and the narrative style rather clumsy, but people didn't care. There were a few particularly juicy sections where Jasmin tore into her parents, especially her father. It was clear from the book that he had lavished money on his daughter but had given her neither his time nor his love. She wrote candidly about her father's many affairs and how her mother had hit back with her own indiscretions. The book sold like hotcakes.

The following year, Jasmin bought an apartment in Vasastan, in the same building where Maud lived. It was the only apartment on the ground floor. It had a special entrance at the foot of the elaborate marble staircase in the lobby, and its windows looked out onto both the street and the backyard. With the permission of the housing association board, the previous owner had built a small glassed-in terrace at the back. He owned an IT company and had renovated the run-down apartment to the highest standards, according to what Maud had heard. When he married and the couple was expecting their first child, he sold the place to Jasmin Schimmerhof and moved to a delightful house by the sea. Among other reasons, Jasmin wanted the apartment because it was fairly large—around 450 square feet. After the success of her autobiography, she had decided to embark on a new career. She was going to be an artist. Several walls were knocked down in order to make room for a substantial studio. Jasmin wanted to create large installations and needed space.

She had spent the entire spring working on her creations. She wrote in her blog, Me Jasmin: *I despise sovereignty and the patriarchy. I have grown up under that kind of oppression, and I know how terrible it is. I want to give the finger to all oppressors and tell them to go to hell! In*

October, I will be putting on an exhibition at the Hell Gallery. Come along and see my new pieces! At the moment I am working on Phallus, Hang-ing. *It's going to be a kick in the balls for all those bastard men!*

Maud had learned all this over the past few weeks by looking up newspaper articles online; she also found Jasmin's blog extremely infor-mative, and it contained high-res pictures of various works. The enormous pieces of art had thickly painted layers of color, into which Jas-min had pressed photographs, scraps of fabric, sheet music, tampons (Maud couldn't quite see whether or not they were used), fragments of bone, and all kinds of unidentifiable trash. And trash was precisely the right word for Jasmin's art, in Maud's opinion. The pictures were titled *No Title I, No Title II, No Title III,* and so on.

Her so-called sculptures all had the same construction. Each one had a concrete base into which Jasmin had stuck various objects before the concrete had set. There were pieces featuring old exhaust systems pointing up at the ceiling, baseball bats, broken ice hockey sticks, golf clubs, cone-shaped items with *Missile* or *Atomic bomb* written on the side, and—last but not least—enormous black rubber dildos. Needless to say, these masterpieces were titled PHALLUS I, PHALLUS II, PHALLUS III, presumably ad infinitum.

Makes life easier, I suppose, Maud thought.

Every morning Maud spent an hour or so surfing the Internet on her laptop, checking out interesting people and events. She hadn't bothered researching Jasmin's life when her flamboyant neighbor moved in; at the time, Maud had been fully occupied with planning her first visit to a spa. After a very successful stay she had gone on vacation to Sardinia, where she had spent three glorious months before returning to Gothenburg.

And that was when it began.

MAUD HAD BEEN home for only a couple of days when the doorbell suddenly rang. Those days it was a rare occurrence, so Maud went to see who was there. Through the peephole she could see a woman standing outside.

Hesitantly, Maud opened the door a fraction of an inch. The woman was slim and dainty, with bleached, tousled hair loosely pulled back in a ponytail on top of her head in a big pink plastic clip. She was smiling brightly, and said in an exaggeratedly loud voice without pausing for breath:

"Hi there! My name is Jasmin Schimmerhof and I moved in here back in the spring. I threw a big housewarming party for all the neighbors in August, but unfortunately you were away, so I thought I'd bring you a little taste of what we ate and drank at the party. May I come in?"

Broadly speaking, everyone Maud met these days spoke loudly and articulated with exaggerated clarity. They automatically assumed she was deaf, which she most definitely was not. Nor was she senile. But she had learned that it was smart not to reveal that all her senses were in full working order; instead, she allowed people to act in accordance with their own preconceptions. This was often a useful source of information, and Maud could form her own opinion of the person and the situation. But this time she didn't exactly adopt her usual approach. Later on, Maud would blame it on the fact that she had been completely taken by surprise. Perhaps there was also a certain amount of curiosity about her famous neighbor. In any case, that was when she made her first mistake. She let her visitor into the apartment.

Jasmin danced in through the door like a playful breeze. The careless ponytail bobbed and swung as she turned her head in all directions, checking out the spacious apartment. A sheer white kaftan billowed around her, with only a tiny tank top underneath; it was obvious she wasn't wearing a bra. Her black leggings were covered in pale dust and little hard lumps of something that looked like dried plaster or cement. Her feet were even dirtier, if that were possible. They were also rather conspicuous because Jasmin had shoved them into a pair of open sandals. Chipped blue nail polish adorned her toenails. She turned around, tilted her head to one side, and gazed appraisingly at the old lady, who was still standing by the door. With

13

another beaming smile she handed over a shiny bright red gift bag.

"There you go. Leftover champagne and caviar. They both need to go in the refrigerator. We actually had shellfish too, but of course it doesn't keep. Where's the kitchen?" she said in a loud, cheerful voice.

Her shining eyes should have warned Maud, but instead she made her second mistake. She accepted the red bag.

"Thank you. But there was really no need . . ." Maud murmured.

"I know. But I thought you ought to FEEL that I'm living here now. That it makes a difference. We're going to be really good friends," Jasmine said in a lighthearted voice, but still at full volume.

Before Maud could stop her, she shot off down the long hallway and found the kitchen door.

"Soooo wonderful, and soooo much space! I'm sure nothing has changed since this place was built at least a hundred years ago, apart from the stove and the refrigerator!"

Jasmin made the comment with a smile to show that she was joking, but Maud picked up something in her tone. She couldn't quite put her finger on what it was, but she knew right away that she didn't like it.

"This really is an enormous apartment. How big is it?" Jasmin asked, still smiling.

"Almost a thousand square feet," Maud answered reluctantly.

It was actually slightly larger, but she thought that was none of Miss Schimmerhof's business.

Jasmin nodded to herself as if she had just received confirmation of something she already knew or had suspected. She gave Maud a speculative glance, but seemed to change her mind.

"I'd better go back downstairs and get on with my work. You're very welcome to come and have a look at my little studio. As I said, it's . . ."

She didn't finish the sentence, but flashed another quick smile. Maud put the red gift bag on the counter and accompanied her uninvited

15

guest to the front door. When they got there, Jasmin turned around and gave her a big hug. Maud could feel Jasmin's soft breasts under her top as they pressed against her own small, flat bosom. She was so taken aback that it didn't occur to her to defend herself. At the same time, she was embarrassed. Nobody had hugged her for several decades. In fact, she couldn't even remember the last time somebody had touched her, apart from the therapists at the Selma Spa Hotel, of course. But that had been entirely professional, rather than an expression of affection.

"See you soon," Jasmin chirped.

Maud had still not recovered from the hug and the confusing feelings it aroused. She caught herself mumbling something in response and nodding in agreement. To think that a hug could knock her off balance so completely!

Without really knowing why, Maud once again had a bad feeling as she listened to Jasmin's footsteps disappearing down the stairs. And yet there was something else there too: a longing for someone to touch her. For someone to smile at her. If only she had known . . . But how could she have known? Jasmin would turn out to be far removed from most things Maud had come across during her long life.

THE CHAMPAGNE WAS a really expensive brand—Champagne de Pompadour. When Maud looked it up on the Internet, she saw that it cost 549 kronor at the state-owned liquor store. Ridiculous! Admittedly, Maud enjoyed the odd glass of genuine champagne from time to time, but she was happy with brands that cost less than half that amount. The little tin of Russian caviar was also the real deal and probably cost as much as the champagne. Maud seriously doubted whether the other residents of the apartment block had been offered such expensive delicacies at Jasmin's housewarming party, which led her to conclude that Jasmin was trying to get into her good books. But why? Perhaps she was lonely and looking for friendship? Maud was an old woman, a good forty-five years older than the social butterfly with artistic ambitions; they had nothing whatsoever in common. What did she want? Was she looking for a surrogate grandmother?

After a little research online, Maud discovered that Jasmin's maternal grandmother was still alive. She seemed to be a lively and active person, and she was two years younger than Maud. It was obvious that both of Jasmin's parents came from wealthy families. Her father was now seventy-six; when he eventually passed away, his new wife would inherit his money, together with Jasmin and her half-sister. The wife would probably be the main beneficiary, but Jasmin would be entitled to her legal share, which would no doubt be substantial.

It's easy to criticize the patriarchy and the upper classes when you come from a privileged background and expect to inherit a fortune, Maud thought to herself, pulling a face. She had had to fight for the very basics for most of her life. She had been able to do quite a bit of traveling after Charlotte's death, but she was forced to take in three tenants in order to make ends meet. This had been possible because the apartment was so large, and she hadn't been at home all that much while she was working. The last tenant had moved out twenty-five years ago, when Maud retired. By that time she had saved enough money to get by for the rest of her life. She had invested a small amount in long-term safe bonds; the income from this investment, together with her small pension, was enough for her simple needs. She also had plenty of money in the bank, which she used when she wanted to travel farther afield, and that money would see her through. There was no one to inherit from her after her death.

It was clear from Maud's research that Jasmin wasn't looking for a surrogate grandmother. So what did she want? Maud thought about that farewell hug. The soft, warm . . . But there was nothing in Jasmin's blog to suggest that she was a lesbian. Quite the reverse. In spite of her frequently expressed hatred of men, she wrote on several occasions about "fantastic one night stands" with young men. The younger the better. No one over thirty, and preferably around twenty. According to one entry, she thought men over thirty were "smelly and boring." She warmly recommended brief relationships with younger men because they didn't involve any kind of commitment. They merely provided an outlet for a woman's sexual desires, as she put it.

There are female chauvinist pigs too, Maud thought.

No, this had nothing to do with surrogate grannies or sex. So what was going on?

BARELY A WEEK later, the doorbell rang again, loud and long. In Maud's world, it felt as if her visitor had only just left. With a sigh she got up from her comfortable armchair and went out into the hallway. She had a feeling she knew who it was. A glance through the spy hole confirmed her suspicions, but still she opened the door. Mistake number three.

"Hi there, Maud! I've made some pastries; I thought we could have coffee together. You do have coffee, don't you? I've just run out."

Maud couldn't quite work out how it had happened, but suddenly Jasmin was standing in the apartment. She bounded off in the direction of the kitchen, leaving in her wake the seductive aroma of freshly baked vanilla pastries. With a sigh, Maud closed the front door.

By the time she reached the kitchen, Jasmin was already filling up the coffee pot with water. The tin of coffee was beside her on the counter. *She's taken that out of the top cupboard by the stove*, Maud thought. With deft movements Jasmin spooned the coffee powder into the Melitta filter, chattering away at the same time.

"I mean, we're both alone and home all day. I'm alone by choice, of course, because I need peace and quiet in order to create. That's the hard part, you know. Coming up with good ideas. Realizing those ideas afterward isn't so much of a problem. Although I do work in large formats. My pictures measure several square feet, but of course I can hang those on the walls. Then again, I don't really have any wall space left. The sculptures and installations are even more difficult. There's not much room; the study is already too small. I publish pictures of my work on the Internet, and I have a blog. Do you know what that means? No? I can show you when you come down to my place. It's brilliant! I've sold several pieces through the blog. And I've got a big exhibition coming up in a few weeks. The private view is on October fifteenth. You will come, won't you?"

At that point Jasmin had to pause for breath. She fixed her big eyes on Maud and tilted her head to one side. Her face might have been marked by the life she had led, but her eyes were an extraordinary shade of blue, and almost innocent. Maud was confused and didn't really know what to say. Automatically she reverted to her role of Very Old Lady.

"Oh, I don't know . . . all those people. I don't usually go to that kind of thing . . ." she said evasively.

"In that case, it's high time you did! I'll pick you up and we can go together in a cab," Jasmin said firmly.

I don't want to see the trash you produce! Maud wanted to scream, but something held

22

her back. Perhaps it was simply her good old-fashioned upbringing. Instead she nodded feebly, which could have meant anything.

"Then it's all arranged!" Jasmin said, interpreting the nod to suit herself.

She rummaged through the kitchen cupboards and found coffee cups and the sugar bowl.

"Do you take milk?" she asked.

Maud shook her head wearily. Before she had time to react, Jasmin had opened the refrigerator and was poking around inside.

"Don't you have any milk?"

"No."

At last Maud was beginning to recover from the intrusion. Because that was exactly what it was: an intrusion into her calm, peaceful world, where she set the pace and rhythm of her day.

"No," she said again, just because it felt good to say no to this person.

They had their coffee and pastries in Maud's small living room, which was where she spent most of her time since the space also functioned as her bedroom. The bathroom was on the other side of the hall. The truth was that Maud used no more than around two hundred square feet of the huge apartment, which Jasmin pointed out after a while. Maud could feel the anger beginning to bubble away inside her. How she lived in her own apartment was of no concern to anyone else. She merely mumbled something unintelligible in response.

Jasmin didn't appear to notice Maud's reserved attitude, but continued to prattle on: "The fact is that the way we live is another thing we have in common. I need space for my art, so I live in two small rooms. Plus the kitchen and bathroom, of course. Just like you! I use the rest of my apartment as a studio. And then of course there's the glassed-in terrace. You really must come down and have a look! Everything is sooooo clean and new!"

Once again Maud played the old lady who was slightly confused, and mumbled something into her cake. Which was in a pleated case with DAHLS KONDITORI printed on it. So much for being homemade!

When she was about to leave, Jasmin stopped just outside the door. She looked at Maud with an expression of deep concern and patted her gently on the cheek. "Isn't it a bit too much for you, having to walk up all these stairs?"

She pointed to the long staircase that led from the main door up to the elevator and Maud's apartment.

"No," said Maud, and shut the door.

JASMIN'S VISITS GREW more and more frequent. She usually brought something tasty to have with their coffee; occasionally she brought a bottle of wine. Maud tried to fend off both the gifts and the visits, but it was as if she were somehow incapable of putting any real strength behind her efforts. Jasmin would simply wave away her protests with a little laugh and a few dance steps. When she was finally ready to leave, she would give Maud a hug or an affectionate pat on the cheek. She always invited Maud down to her apartment.

"You just have to see my place! It's absolutely FANTASTIC!"

But Maud always responded evasively. She still hadn't worked out what it was that Jasmin wanted from her. Did she seek out Maud's company because she herself was lonely? Or was she playing the Good Samaritan, taking care of a lonely old lady? Or . . . or what?

It wasn't until she read a new entry in Jasmin's blog one day that things started to become clear. *I'm so excited! I might soon be moving into a bigger apartment! Which means a bigger studio, of course!!!! I really need more space. And when I say bigger, I mean BIGGER! MUCH BIGGER!!!*

So that was the reason for Jasmin's intense charm offensive. The intrusion, the way she forced herself on her neighbor . . . Maud felt quite stunned as she sat there, her anger rising. She took a few deep breaths to clear her mind.

That little bitch was after her apartment.

The first autumn gale was blowing up outside the window, and yellow leaves danced against the glass. It was starting to drizzle; there was no doubt that a real storm was on the way. Maud switched off all the lights and settled back down in her armchair. The darkness crept out of every corner, slowly filling the room. If Jasmin turned up, Maud had no intention of opening the door. She needed to think.

The shrill sound of the doorbell sliced through the silence. Maud didn't move a muscle. She knew that the bell would ring again. And again. And again. Eventually, Jasmin gave up. Her footsteps disappeared in the direction of the cellar stairs and the door leading out into the back yard. A heavy thud echoed through the stairwell as the door closed behind her. Maud was sitting a short distance away from the window so that she couldn't be seen from the yard; there were no lights on, so Jasmin would assume she had gone out, or was having a little nap.

Needless to say, it was all because the "artist" couldn't buy her apartment in the usual way. No doubt she was used to fixing everything with her money, but in this case it wouldn't work. Maud didn't own the apartment; she simply had the right to live there for as long as she wished. She had lived in these rooms for eighty-eight years, and she wasn't about to move now. But what did

Jasmin have up her sleeve? Presumably she was planning some kind of swap. She had already asked Maud if the stairs weren't a bit much for her; she had pointed out that the apartment was old-fashioned and unnecessarily large; several times she had mentioned that her studio was too small for her monumental works of art, and now there was this latest blog entry where she sounded sure of victory. These were clear indications of Jasmin's intentions, and Maud knew she wouldn't give up until she had forced the exchange of apartments, one way or another. That spoiled upper-class bitch wasn't accustomed to not getting her own way. Perhaps she would appeal to the housing association board? There were no doubt plenty of board members who were less than happy that Maud was occupying such a valuable space without paying any rent. If Jasmin said she felt sorry for the old lady who was getting a bit senile and finding it difficult to manage in that big apartment . . . and that she was willing to swap so Maud wouldn't have to struggle with the stairs, and could have a more disability-friendly place . . . She would probably present her case as if she were making the offer out of sheer thoughtfulness toward her elderly neighbor. If anyone could pull it off, it was Jasmin. For a moment, Maud considered simply going away for a few months. To Mexico, or . . . she stopped right there. No, she had to stay put and protect her interests. If she wasn't here, Jasmin would have free rein. Who knew what she would say to the other residents and the housing association board?

For the first time in her long life, Maud felt weak and powerless, but after a while her brain began to function as it always did in a crisis. An idea began to take shape. After examining it thoroughly from all angles, she made up her mind.

It was time to pay Jasmin a visit.

MAUD PICKED UP her sturdy stick in her right hand; in her left hand she carried the bag of trash from her kitchen, and under her arm she had tucked a bundle of old newspapers. She made her way down to the garbage containers in the lobby. She placed the newspapers in one of the big plastic recycling bins and dropped the trash in the container labeled LANDFILL. She thought all that business of sorting the trash into "compostable" and "landfill" was nonsense.

She then made her way to Jasmin's front door, which was unusually robust and was reinforced with a broad band of steel all the way around. Maud could see three separate keyholes. She supposed that kind of thing might be necessary if you lived on the ground floor, even if the main door of the apartment block was always locked. She rang the bell, and heard a *ding dong* that sounded like a cathedral bell. The sound was muffled by the heavy door, but Maud could still hear it clearly. After a while the door opened and Jasmin peered out through the gap. When she saw who it was, she slipped off the security chain and opened the door wide.

"Maud! I'm so pleased you're here at last!" She beamed, sounding as if she really meant it.

For a moment, Maud wavered. Could she have made a mistake? Perhaps Jasmin really liked her and wasn't after her apartment at all.

"Let me show you my beautiful apartment!

It's modern and comfortable—I know you're going to LOVE it!"

Every trace of doubt disappeared from Maud's mind. Her suspicions had been well-founded; as usual, Jasmin was trying to sell the advantages of her apartment.

In her feeblest and most timid voice, Maud said, "I'm sorry . . . I hope I'm not disturbing you. I just brought the trash down and I thought . . ."

"Of course not. Come on in! I've been asking you to drop by and have a look around!"

"But I haven't brought anything with me . . . I just rang the bell on impulse . . ."

"For Heaven's sake! The most important thing is that you're here!" Jasmin danced away down the hall, beckoning Maud inside.

Before crossing the threshold, Maud glanced out into the backyard, and checked the windows in the lobby. There wasn't a soul in sight. She quickly stepped inside, and the heavy door closed behind her.

The hallway was quite large and gloomy. Along one wall were closets with mirrored sliding doors. On the opposite wall hung a large piece of art in dark colors. It was impossible to make out what had been pressed into the paint because the lighting was so poor, but it appeared to be torn-out newspaper articles. The only source of illumination was a small wall light that looked like a lump of cement with a naked bulb stuck in the middle. Probably something Jasmin had made. Chattering away happily, she led Maud into the kitchen, which was a futuristic dream in glass and stainless steel. The windows overlooked the backyard; Maud was careful to stay away from them. A doorway led to the small glassed-in terrace.

"During the spring and summer I always eat out there; because it's glassed-in, the weather doesn't matter. But isn't the kitchen FANTAS-TIC? The induction stove cooks your food in no time!" Jasmin assured her visitor.

Maud had installed her electric oven at the same time as her combined refrigerator and freezer. That would have been in . . . 1983. Or possibly 1984. Both worked perfectly well, and she had absolutely no interest in something that cooked her food "in no time." Firstly, she rarely cooked; she bought most of her provisions from the local ICA Gourmet store, which sold ready meals that could simply be heated up in the oven or microwave. They were prepared in a restaurant kitchen just a few miles away. Occasionally, she might heat up a tin of soup. And secondly, she already found it difficult enough to make sure things didn't burn. Several times she had forgotten about a pan on the heat. With the speed of this induction stove, she would probably burn everything. No, she wasn't interested in anything like that. But she didn't say so. Instead she opened her eyes wide and said:

"Goodness me . . ."

"The kitchen's amazing, isn't it? And it's so practical and easy to clean!"

Jasmin sounded like an over-enthusiastic real estate agent. Which perhaps she was, in a way.

"And wait until you see the bathroom!"

She disappeared into the hallway, with

33

Maud trailing slowly behind. The huge bathroom also sent shivers down her spine. It was covered from floor to ceiling in black and white tiles, with gold faucets and a gigantic corner bath.

"Look, it's a Jacuzzi!" Jasmin said with the same enthusiasm she had lavished on the kitchen.

"Oooh," Maud murmured, trying to look impressed.

Both the kitchen and the bathroom were appalling. The bedroom and the small living room were even worse, if that was possible. There was nothing in the bedroom apart from a huge circular bed in the middle of the floor. It was unmade and Maud could see that the black sheets were made of some kind of shiny fabric. The living room was entirely white. The only pieces of furniture were a big white sofa and an oval coffee table that appeared to be made of wrought iron. The rug was white and kind of shaggy. Some of Jasmin's pieces were displayed on the walls. One of them had lots of wine bottle labels pushed into the paint, while another had several hash pipes stuck to it. Maud had been to India often enough to recognize a hash pipe when she saw one.

"Ta-da! My studio! The vinyl flooring has been put down to cover a really beautiful oak floor, so all you have to do is lift it up, and there you go!"

Jasmin led Maud into the large room. There were pieces on every wall; Maud had already seen them on Jasmin's blog. She also recognized the various "Phallus" sculptures on the floor. There was only one that she hadn't seen on the blog. It was hanging from the ceiling. Jasmin guided Maud around her work, explaining at length that she was "striving to unmask the domineering tactics of the patriarchy." Maud contented herself with the odd "oooh" or "I see" at appropriate points; otherwise she kept quiet.

Eventually they reached the final piece: the sculpture suspended from the ceiling.

"This is my latest project. It's almost finished. It's called *Phallus, Hanging*. That's why I've hoisted it up to the ceiling. I want it to hang like this. But it's also because I'm so short of space on the floor."

"I see," Maud murmured again.

The actual framework of the piece was a large old-fashioned wagon wheel made of wood. Using strong steel wire, Jasmin had attached penises of different sizes and of varying appearance to the spokes. They were also made of a range of materials; several of the largest ones were cast in bronze, some were made of clay, others of concrete. There were even some bright red and green ones. The wheel was suspended by a block-and-tackle mechanism from a sturdy hook in the ceiling. The rope ran through the tackle and was tied to the thick pipe leading to the radiator. On the wall Jasmin had mounted the kind of trigger-release shackle used on sailboats to fix the sheet to the sail. It was an impressive device made of black rubber. Maud pointed to the shackle, her finger trembling slightly.

"Is that really strong enough to hold the weight of the whole thing? I mean . . . if you unfasten the rope?" she asked timidly.

"Yes indeed! I bought it in an ordinary

chandlery. It's big enough to hold the sail on a racing yacht in a gale. It's exactly what I need, because it's holding up a considerable weight, just like the weight of a sail. When I want to add a new cock—excuse my language, but that's what they are—I need to be able to control the speed when I lower the wheel. The shackle means I can lock it at a comfortable height so that I can easily work on it. The hook was already in place; there used to be a massive chandelier in here. The ceiling height is around sixteen feet, after all."

Maud's ceiling was the same height; a plan was beginning to take shape in her head. She opened her eyes wide and said, "But it looks impossible! I mean, those . . . those things . . . the ones in bronze . . . must be incredibly heavy!"

"They sure are. But watch . . . the shackle can take the weight."

Jasmin went over to the radiator, bent down and undid the knot. Now only the trigger-release shackle was holding up *Phallus, Hanging*. Maud felt her pulse rate increase slightly, but controlled herself and pointed to one of the bright green penises.

37

"What's that one made of?" she asked.

"It's just Play-Doh, the stuff kids use in nursery school. It's a soft modeling material that you harden in the oven at a low temperature."

"And what about that one?"

Maud pointed indiscriminately toward one side of the wheel.

"Which one? Do you mean the concrete cocks, or . . . ?"

"I'm not sure . . . that one," Maud said vaguely.

She was still pointing upward as she slowly edged closer to the rope. Jasmin went over to her masterpiece, trying to work out which of the male attributes Maud was wondering about. She ended up standing directly beneath the wheel, gazing upwards. Perfect! Maud jerked the rope as hard as she could, and the shackle released it immediately.

With a deafening crash, *Phallus, Hanging* landed right on top of Jasmin. She didn't even have time to make a sound.

Afterward an eerie silence filled the room. Maud held her breath as she listened for the sound of running footsteps, but she didn't hear a thing. The neighbors were probably used to strange noises coming from Jasmin's apartment. Quickly she moved over to the motionless body on the floor. A substantial pool of blood was beginning to seep out from underneath the wagon wheel. Through the wooden spokes Maud could see that Jasmin's skull had been crushed by one of the bronze penises.

The patriarchy strikes back, she thought.

She headed for the hallway as quickly as possible. She had been very careful not to touch anything during the tour of the apartment, so she didn't need to waste time wiping off any possible fingerprints. She pressed her ear to the front door to check whether there was anyone in the lobby or the yard, but there wasn't a sound to suggest that this might be the case. She pulled the sleeve of her cardigan over her right hand before she pressed down the handle and cautiously edged opened the door and peeked out. There was no one around. She slipped out and closed the door behind her; she heard the lock click into place.

LATER THAT EVENING Maud became aware of a certain amount of activity in the street. When she looked out of the window she saw an ambulance and two police cars with flashing blue lights parked outside the main door of the building. Maud was hidden behind the curtain; no one could see her in the dark room.

After almost an hour the paramedics came out carrying a stretcher. They had covered the face of the person they were carrying; *a sure sign that the person is dead*, Maud thought.

She didn't feel any sense of triumph, merely a calm serenity. Now no one would threaten her home. She would live there for the rest of her life. At the same time, there was another feeling. It took a while before she managed to identify it. Emptiness. Loss, perhaps. Was that possible? Apparently so.

Well, I can live with that, Maud thought.

She moved away from the window and into the darkness.

(2012)

M AUD WAS FOUR months later than usual. Normally her travel plans for the summer were sorted out by January, but this year she still hadn't made up her mind where to go. It was probably because of her age. Not that she suffered from any mental or physical frailty; quite the reverse. She had visited the local clinic about a month ago to ask for some medication for a mild bout of conjunctivitis. The young doctor, who didn't even look old enough to have graduated from high school, pointed out with amazement that it had been sixteen years since her last visit. And on that occasion she had gone for an anti-jaundice vaccination that was supposed to provide long-lasting protection.

She had assured the doctor several times that she felt absolutely fine. In spite of her protests, he had insisted on giving her a thorough examination and had instructed the nurse to take blood samples. A complete waste of time. She was as fit as a fiddle, she had kept on telling him. Although she had to admit that the ointment the young doctor had prescribed had cleared up the problem with her eye.

No, the reason why she still hadn't firmed up her travel plans was she had already been virtually all over the world. She had visited the pyramids in Egypt, clambered up an Inca temple in the Andes, floated like a cork in the Dead Sea, and walked along the Great Wall of China. She had even been to Greenland and the South Pole. She had already seen and experienced everything that was worth seeing and experiencing.

During the last fifteen years of her teaching career, she had traveled the globe during her summer vacations. After her retirement, she had spent the whole year visiting different places, spending only short periods at home. She had had a lot of catching up to do.

After the death of her parents, she had been left to take care of her mentally ill sister. Only after Charlotte's death almost forty years ago had it become possible for Maud to get away.

Maud had just started college when her father died. She often thought that the period before his death had been the happiest of her life, not least because she had just gotten engaged. On her eighteenth birthday, her engagement to Lieutenant Gustaf Adelsiöö was announced. She remembered floating on a little cloud of pure joy, mainly because she was going to marry Gustaf, whom she really believed that she loved. However, almost-equally compelling to Maud was the thought of getting away from her over-anxious mother and her fragile sister.

Charlotte had been eleven years older than Maud. As time went by, she developed a range of phobias and a debilitating hypochondria that gradually took over her life. No man had ever proposed to her, and her parents realized it was never going to happen.

Therefore, they were very pleased Maud was going to marry a young man from a good family.

Shortly after her father's death, Gustaf had sent a letter in which he broke off the engagement in no uncertain terms. Maud didn't doubt for a moment that his mother and father had been behind the painful words. It was well-known that the Adelsiöö family were of noble descent, even though their fortune had diminished significantly over the past two decades—which coincided with when Gustaf's father had been the head of the family. He had no skill with either goods or money—not that he would ever admit it—and he continued with his extravagant lifestyle, treating other people with condescension. The only reason why Gustaf's parents had accepted his engagement to Maud was they believed her father was rich. When his death revealed that he was bankrupt, that was a good enough reason to break off the engagement immediately, according to Gustaf's parents.

Of course Maud had cried a great deal during the days after the letter arrived, but it wasn't really because of a broken heart. Her greatest disappointment was that she wasn't going to be able to leave home.

One week later, Hitler's troops marched into Poland, and the Second World War broke out.

Maud soon had more serious problems to deal with than a broken engagement. Her mother was utterly devastated by the sudden death of Maud's father, and by the realization that there was no money. She stayed in bed all day, refusing to get up. During the first months of the war, she began to fade away, and two years later she was dead. The previous year, Maud had completed her training and managed to get a job at the local all-girls' high school. She took on all the overtime available in order to provide for herself, her mother, and her sister. Things got a little easier after her mother passed away, particularly as Maud managed to use her mother's ration card and coupons for a full twelve months after her death. On several occasions during the war and the years that followed, Maud had suggested to her sister that they should take in one or more tenants since they certainly had the room to do so. Every time, Charlotte became terribly upset. She would walk around the desolate rooms, whimpering and wringing her hands. "I can't cope with strangers! I don't want strangers living here! I'll just *die* if you bring strangers into my home!" she would sob in despair. Sometimes she would work herself up into a paroxysm of hysteria. Afterward she always wanted more pills than her doctor had prescribed, and Maud would try to resist. However, she didn't always have the strength. It was lovely and peaceful when her sister was asleep. That was the only time Maud had to herself in those days. Traveling was out of the question. Charlotte never set foot outside the door.

Over all the years that Maud had overseen their joint finances, she had deposited the whole of her sister's sickness benefit into a special bank account. As time went by, it had grown into a tidy little sum, and after Charlotte's death, Maud also rented out three of the rooms in the spacious apartment, and turned her sister's room into a small kitchen diner for the use of the residents, who also shared the biggest bathroom. She saved the rent, thinking that it would provide a decent pension eventually.

It had now been twenty-five years since Maud had retired and stopped taking on tenants, and she had visited most of the countries in the world. And she had no idea where she wanted to go this summer.

India was too hot, Nice too noisy, while the air quality was very poor in both Paris and New York. Bali, perhaps? Or possibly Sardinia, her favorite Mediterranean island? But she had already been to all these places several times. Was there somewhere new that she hadn't thought of? She couldn't come up with anything. *Maybe I'm getting a bit indecisive*, she thought with a sigh.

Maud was a seasoned tourist who traveled light. The feeling she got when she set off with a one-way plane ticket was wonderful. She usually followed the itinerary she had worked out in advance, but she rarely booked overnight accommodation or journeys between the places she wanted to visit. If she found somewhere she liked, she could stay there for as long as she wished. It was quite lonely traveling that way, but it didn't bother her; it was the way she wanted it. No pointless chatter and no complaining. She made her own decisions.

Maud put some coffee on and went into the hallway to pick up the newspaper, *Göteborgs-Posten*. She always read it while she was having her breakfast, more out of habit than anything else. When she had finished the paper she would switch on her laptop and spend a while surfing the net, where she could get a quick update on what was happening out there in the big wide world. These days she usually found cheap flights online too. Her laptop was indispensable. She had acquired it after the Silver Surfers IT course she had taken eight years prior. She had enrolled in Charlotte's name. When the course was over they were supposed to hand in their laptops, but Maud had simply ignored the reminders. Eventually a letter arrived threatening to take legal action; only then did Maud send a brief reply:

> *Dear Tutor,*
>   *I am very sorry to inform you that my sister Charlotte unexpectedly passed away three weeks ago. I have not found a computer among her possessions.*
>   *Yours sincerely,*
>   *Maud Adelsiöö*

She used her ex-fiancé's noble surname in order to command greater respect, and it had obviously worked because she received no more requests to return the laptop.

Maud toasted two slices of bread and spread them with a thin layer of marmalade as usual, then she placed slices of mature Greve cheese on top. She boiled an egg for precisely three minutes. Her breakfast had been exactly the same for the last forty years. Before that it had been porridge every morning because Charlotte wouldn't eat anything else.

Maud stirred a little hot milk into the strong coffee and carried her tray into the TV room. With a contented sigh she sank down into the big armchair that had belonged to her father. Slowly and methodically she began to read the paper, starting from the first page as she always did. The only part she skipped was the sports section.

When she reached the family announcements page, her attention was caught by a headline: *It's never too late for love, says Gustaf, 90, as he marries Zazza, 55.*

When she saw the picture of the smiling couple, her mind went completely blank. She couldn't process what the writing said. It couldn't be true! The man in the picture was her Gustaf. And she knew exactly who the woman was too. She took a few deep breaths in order to slow her racing pulse, then she began to read.

According to the article, after being a

widower for five years, Gustaf Adelsiöö had met the actress Zazza Henrix on a Mediterranean cruise last fall. They got engaged on New Year's Eve, and now they were getting married the day before Whitsunday.

After the wedding the happy couple is intending to move into the groom's family estate, Ekenäs manor house outside Sunne in Värmland. The wedding is being celebrated at the Selma Spa. The exclusive hotel will take care of all the practical arrangements, leaving the bride and groom to enjoy their special day to the full, together with family and friends.

When she read those final sentences, Maud felt quite ill. This wasn't good. It wasn't good at all! She knew considerably more than the journalist who had written the article. And doubtless more than poor Gustaf.

She had discreetly followed Gustaf's life over the years. He had married a wealthy girl from Värmland, so Ekenäs was her family estate, not his. They had had two children, but the boy tragically died from leukemia when he was only ten years old. The daughter trained to be a dentist and married a colleague. Maud knew that they had three children, all of whom were now grown up and had left the nest. She also knew that Gustaf's daughter and her husband ran a dental practice together in Torsby. They lived on the Ekenäs estate. Gustaf and his now late wife had moved away ten years ago when she fell ill, but obviously he and his wife-to-be were planning to take over the estate.

Maud knew his fiancée all too well, and she had no doubt who was behind that decision.

Zazza Henrix was called Siv Hansson back in the days when Maud was her teacher, and even then Maud thought she was a full-fledged trollop. She frequently played truant and didn't give a damn about her schoolwork. Nor did she care much when she was reprimanded. She also belonged to the gang that sneaked off for a smoke during recess. Makeup, clothes, and boys were the only things that interested her. As a result, her grades were poor, but that didn't seem to bother her. When the school's career adviser asked with some concern whether she had any plans for the future, fifteen-year-old Siv had replied with absolute conviction, "I'm going to be an actress!"

Maud lost track of Siv for a few years, but one morning she unexpectedly turned up in the newspaper; there was a big picture of her, posing stark naked. Underneath the picture it said that Siv, who had already changed her name to Zazza Henrix, was a glamour model and the star of a Swedish soft-core porn film that was soon to be released. The film was a flop. From then on, Maud had followed Siv from a distance, which was something she did with *certain individuals* she felt it was worth keeping an eye on, for various reasons. The little laptop had proved extremely useful when it came to keeping abreast of what people were doing and saying, so she knew that Siv's film career had more or less died after that first film. During the next few years she had played minor roles in a range of por-nos, but she never became a big name.

Sometimes Siv would turn up in the gossip columns, usually involved in some scandal or other. She had married a little-known film director, but they divorced after only twelve months or so. She had had lots of different relationships, but no children.

Maud went over to the bookcase and took out a file marked *Students*. She turned to the letter *H* in the index. Neatly stored in plastic wallets was every single article she had gathered from the Internet and newspapers about Siv Hansson, alias Zazza Henrix. She quickly skimmed through them, then resolutely picked up her cell phone. It was time to book her first trip of the summer. She had never actually visited a spa during her long life.

EASTER HAD BEEN late this year, and therefore Whitsun was late too. It was a warm, sunny day at the beginning of June when she arrived in Sunne. A cab picked up Maud and two other guests at the train station. Her fellow passengers were a couple in their sixties who were obviously married. They didn't exchange a single word during the short drive to the hotel. Maud's luggage consisted of a suitcase and a sturdy stick with a rubber spike on the end. The stick had been leaning against the wall by the door of the clinic when she went to see the doctor about the problem with her eye. She had picked it up on the way out. *You never know when something like this might come in handy*, she had thought.

THE HOTEL WAS situated high on a hill and offered a fantastic view of Lake Fryken. The building was narrow, with a long façade; it had been specially designed so that every room looked out over the lake.

Inside, everything was a little too modern for Maud's taste, but she had to admit that her room was very clean and pleasant. She had prudently booked a number of treatments in advance: a facial, massage, manicure, pedicure, and an herbal bath. She had never tried any of them before, so it was probably time she did!

She spent the whole of Thursday afternoon going from one treatment to the next; she swam in the heated pool and relaxed in a sauna. She had forgotten her old swimsuit but bought a new one at reception. She realized that aqua-aerobics wasn't for her. The big pool was extremely crowded, and people were jumping up and down like idiots, splashing water all over the place as they were urged on by brisk exhortations from an extremely fit instructor standing on the side, tightly encased in Lycra.

Maud had booked full board, so she made the most of the delicious food. That night she enjoyed a deep and dreamless sleep in a lovely bed.

FRIDAY MORNING SHE went for her final treatments, the manicure and pedicure. As she left the beautifully scented salon, her fingernails and toenails shimmered in pale pink mother-of-pearl. *Why in God's name have I never done this before?* Maud thought.

Dressed in a new white blouse and a dark blue pencil skirt, she made her entrance into the dining room, leaning on her stick just a little. In spite of the fact that she was prepared, she stopped dead and caught her breath when she saw Siv Hansson, now known as Zazza Henrix, sitting at a table with a woman and a much older man.

Maud's heart flipped over. The slightly stooping, bald-headed man was her Gustaf. He was smartly dressed in light-colored pants and a blue blazer. As he raised his glass of white wine in a toast to his companions, she noticed that his thin hand was shaking. *We've gotten old, you and I*, she thought tenderly. But it was no good standing there getting sentimental. She had an important job to do. It was time to focus.

She went over to the splendid buffet and helped herself. She balanced her full plate carefully on her left hand, using her right to support herself with the stick. She reminded herself to limp.

There was an empty seat at the table adjacent to Gustaf and his ladies. Maud asked the people sitting there if she might join them, and they nodded and smiled. As they chatted amongst themselves, Maud gathered that they intended to have a little rest to allow their lunch to digest before the African dance class began at two o'clock.

The spot she had chosen was perfect. She was free to observe Zazza and her friend. They were so alike that Maud began to suspect they were sisters. Both had medium-length bleached blonde hair. They were heavily made-up, even if they weren't plastered with quite as much as Siv had worn as a teenager. Her thin summer dress was extremely low-cut, revealing the valley between her ample breasts. Were they due to the generosity of nature? Hardly. More likely the work of a skilled cosmetic surgeon. His handiwork was also apparent in Zazza's facial features, which were considerably sharper and more well-defined than those of the woman Maud took to be her sister. Her face seemed somehow slack, in the process of disintegrating. She was probably older than Zazza and couldn't afford a facelift, Maud thought.

It was clear that the three people at the next table had already consumed several glasses of wine during lunch. They were in high spirits, laughing and proposing a series of toasts. Gustaf's head started to nod, and the two women got to their feet. They helped him out of his chair, and with one woman on either side of him, Gustaf left the dining room. Maud pretended not to notice them, but her heart beat a little faster when they walked past her table. None of them so much as glanced in her direction.

She stayed on for a little while and had some dessert. On her way down to the lobby bar for a cup of coffee, she stopped by the front desk. The receptionist was busy checking in a large party that had arrived on a Norwegian tour bus, so Maud discreetly picked up a copy of *Expressen* that was lying on the counter. This was partly because she wanted to glance through the day's news and partly because a newspaper was useful to hide behind.

She didn't have to wait long before the two women emerged from the elevator. Both had changed into white bathrobes and were carrying large towels. They shuffled over to the bar in their complimentary terrycloth slippers, laughing loudly at some joke. Zazza flirted with the young barman as she ordered two large, strong beers. Quietly Maud got up from her armchair as the two women disappeared down the stairs to the pool. She took the elevator up to her room and quickly got changed. On her way out she picked up the stick. Wearing her swimsuit, bathrobe, and slippers, she stepped back into the elevator and went down to the pool area, where she looked exactly like all the other guests.

Zazza and the other woman were sitting in the changing room drinking their beers. From their conversation, Maud gathered that they were disappointed that neither of the Jacuzzis next to the large swimming pool were free. Apparently the plan had been to drink their beer while enjoying the bubbles. She also discovered that the other woman was named Kicki. Without looking at the two of them, Maud placed her bathrobe and slippers in a locker. She showered and adjusted her new swimsuit before slowly making her way toward the door leading to the pool area. She held the stick in a firm grip and remembered to walk with a slight limp. She propped the stick against the wall and clambered down into the pleasantly warm water.

She was swimming up and down the deserted pool at a steady pace when Zazza and Kicki emerged from the changing room. They leapt into the water, giggling and splashing around like little girls. They didn't do much in the way of swimming, but spent most of their time standing at the side gossiping. Maud picked up the odd sentence as she swam past: ". . . his fucking daughter is coming tomorrow . . . she's actually seven years older than me . . ." Zazza said with a meaningful smirk.

Kicki screamed with laughter. "She must be fucking . . . furious!" she managed to gasp between bursts of hilarity.

Maud had heard enough and climbed out of the water. She was so angry that she almost left her stick behind.

Back in the changing room she took a long shower. When she heard the raucous voices of the two women approaching the door, she quickly slipped into the sauna. It was spacious, with plenty of room for at least twenty people. Maud went right to the back and spread her towel on the bottom bench. She had taken the stick in with here. She sat down and tried to relax.

After a little while, Zazza and Kicki came in. Neither of them took any notice of the dried-up old lady sitting at the back.

Zazza sniggered and said, "I'm going to make sure he falls asleep right after dinner. He's not up to much in the bedroom department, if you know what I mean." She winked, and they both burst out laughing again.

"Brilliant! Then we can go down to the bar, and on to the nightclub." Kicki snorted.

Poor Gustaf; it's just as I suspected, Maud thought. But she didn't move a muscle over in her corner.

"I'll go get us a couple more beers," Zazza said.

"That's what I like to hear!" Kicki bellowed.

Both women got to their feet, swaying slightly. For a moment Maud was afraid they were both going to go to the bar, but she was relieved to see that Kicki was merely rearranging her towel so that she could lie down on her back. With a long sigh, she settled down on the bench. By the time the sauna door closed behind Zazza, Kicki was already snoring gently. Maud stood up cautiously and slid out the door.

As it was still lunchtime, the changing room was empty. Right next to the sauna was a small round pool full of ice-cold water, no more than six feet in diameter. Maud tested the temperature with a toe and decided with a shudder that she wouldn't want to get in there. But perhaps it would fit in perfectly with her plan. She quickly ran through the scenario in her mind. This could be the chance she had been waiting for. All she had to do now was to make her preparations and wait for exactly the right moment.

Maud went into the nearest shower cubicle, which was only a couple of feet from the cold pool, and began gently soaping her body. She propped the stick against the wall within easy reach.

A minute or so later, she heard the changing

room door open. For a few terrifying seconds she thought it might be someone other than Zazza, but when she cautiously peeped out she saw that it was indeed her unsuspecting victim, carrying a large plastic cup of beer in each hand. She was concentrating hard on not spilling and didn't notice Maud's head, which quickly disappeared back into the shower.

Maud gripped the stick firmly in both hands. When she could see the distorted outline of her victim through the opaque glass tiles, she prepared herself for the attack. Zazza was only a few steps away from the sauna door when Maud stepped out behind her. Before Zazza had time to turn her head, the old woman whacked her hard on the hip with the rubber spike on the end of her stick. Because Zazza was holding the beers in her hands, she was unable to save herself as she fell, and her head hit the low edge surrounding the small pool with a horrible thud. She lay there with one arm and one leg dangling in the icy water. Maud quickly shoved the rest of the body into the pool, making sure it ended up facedown. With the tip of the stick between her victim's shoulder blades, she kept Zazza underwater for several minutes. Only then did Maud remove the stick and begin to scream.

"Help! Help! She must have tripped! Help!"

Her cries echoed between the tiled walls, and after a little while she heard someone moving inside the sauna.

When Kicki, still half-asleep, managed to get the door open, she saw a naked old woman pointing at the cold pool with her stick and yelling:

"Grab hold of the stick! Here . . . grab the stick!"

Kicki staggered over to the round pool, and soon there were two of them shouting for help.

EVERYTHING HAD GONE exactly according to plan. Several members of the staff came rushing in when they heard the two women shrieking in the changing room. In the middle of all the confusion, a young girl took pity on the bewildered old lady who was sobbing by the edge of the pool, wrapped only in her towel.

The girl gently led Maud to her locker and made sure she put on her bathrobe and slippers. Maud thanked the helpful young lady, who gave her a consoling pat on the cheek before returning to her duties. Maud grabbed the stick once more and limped back to the scene of the accident. Because it was indeed a tragic accident, everyone was agreed on that. Poor Zazza Henrix had lost her footing on the slippery floor and fallen into the ice-cold pool. She had been unlucky in the way she had fallen and struck her head on the edge, fracturing her skull. On the surface of the water, colored red by her blood, two beer cups bobbed up and down—clear evidence that her balance may have been impaired—especially if she had been dehydrated from the sauna.

A man who introduced himself as Head of Security at the hotel came over to ask Maud if she could tell him how the accident had happened. She told him she had been in the shower, and therefore hadn't seen the woman fall.

"My hearing isn't very good, and I had soap in my eyes. And the shower was running, so I didn't hear anything. But maybe I sensed something because suddenly I noticed her lying in the water. I . . . oh my goodness . . . sorry, I can't stop crying . . . that poor woman . . . she was just lying there in the water. I couldn't help her . . . she wouldn't grab hold of my stick . . . all that blood . . . that poor, poor . . ." she sobbed.

He patted her awkwardly on the arm and left her alone.

GUSTAF'S DAUGHTER HAD come to pick him up a few hours after the death of his fiancée. He seemed confused, and his expression was blank. Maud suspected that he was unlikely to pursue his plan to return to Ekenäs; his daughter looked anything but upset.

Maud stayed on for two more days. It might have taken her almost an entire lifetime to pay her first visit to a spa, but she knew it wouldn't be her last. She ate and drank very well. During the day she went for long walks on the forest trails just outside the hotel. Every morning and evening she went for a swim in the heated pool, and after her evening dip she hit the sauna. Needless to say, she never gave Zazza a thought.

Before it was time to go home, Maud made her mind up about her summer vacation. She found a last-minute bargain trip to her beloved Sardinia on the Internet. A cheap hotel was included for the first week, but it was the flight she was after. She knew several wonderful small boarding houses on the island and was pleased to discover that a new luxury spa hotel had been built by the sea just outside Porto Torres. She would be able to book a reservation for a few days if she felt like it. Perhaps she would stay right up until the end of September. Or maybe even longer.

Only time will tell, thought Maud.

(2012)

AN

ELDERLY

LADY

SEEKS

PEACE AT

CHRISTMASTIME

T HE CHURCHYARD WAS silent and peaceful so early on the morning of Christmas Eve. Maud couldn't help but sigh loudly as she struggled along the snow-covered path. It didn't matter because she was all alone. At this time of day there wasn't a living soul in sight, and she was unlikely to disturb the others. The rubber wheels of her walker twisted sideways as she plowed through the deep snow, but after a certain amount of difficulty, she eventually managed to park it next to the grave. She took a couple of special graveside lanterns and a box of matches out of the bag in the wheeled walker's wire basket. Two lanterns on the family grave would have to do—one for her parents and one for her sister. Such things were expensive these days.

Maud had been a late arrival; she had come

along eleven years after Charlotte's birth, much to her parents' surprise and her sister's disgust. Being an only child had suited Charlotte perfectly; a little sister definitely wasn't on her wish list.

Maud suddenly thought back to the lavish parties her parents used to throw. In particular, she remembered the big party they traditionally hosted on New Year's Eve. She recalled the delicious food, the candles burning brightly in the tall candelabra, the champagne corks popping at midnight, the hum of cheerful voices, the smell of cigars and expensive perfume. And of course the beautiful dresses the ladies wore.

Everything had come to an abrupt end when her darling father suffered a heart attack during an Odd Fellows meeting. He had collapsed in the middle of a guffaw after someone told a funny story.

For a number of reasons, Maud's mother had very little to laugh about after his death. Her mother was fifteen years younger than her father, and ought to have been able to forge on, but it was as if all the strength had simply drained out of her and been buried along with him. Two years later, she too was dead. Maud often thought that the shame of their financial and social disgrace had probably broken her mother. She herself had been eighteen when the fatal blow struck her family; she had just started college, where she was training to be a teacher of English and French.

A year or so earlier, Charlotte had developed what her mother referred to as "nerves." Apparently Charlotte was "a sensitive, artistic soul." Although she was a trained pianist, she had never performed in public. Nor could she cope with teaching the piano at home.

The limited amount of capital that was left after the sale of the property diminished rapidly during the war. Maud's teaching salary was barely enough to cover costs. Of course, being able to live rent-free certainly helped their situation, but they still had to pay the utility bills for the large space. Maud remembered how bitterly cold the apartment had been during those terrible winters. The ice that had formed on the inside of the windows was so thick they couldn't see out. They lived in the kitchen and the bedroom next door, keeping the doors tightly closed to retain any warmth. The other rooms were left unheated.

The flickering flames of the candles illuminated the worn inscription on the tall gravestone. Charlotte had died thirty-seven years ago. Only then had Maud's own life begun. *Better late than never*, she thought.

The cold nipping at her toes brought her back to the present. Her boots were warm, but the lining was getting thin and threadbare. Perhaps it was time to buy a new pair.

She began to laboriously maneuver the walker toward the path, which had not been cleared. Heavy snow had fallen overnight. When she listened carefully, she could hear a distant rumble that sounded as if it might be a tractor. A harsh scraping confirmed her suspicions; the snow plow was on its way. She congratulated herself on the fact that there was nothing wrong with her hearing. Most of her contemporaries were practically deaf. But not Maud. Which was perhaps a shame. If she had

been deaf, she wouldn't have been troubled by
The Problem.

Resolutely, she pushed all thoughts of The
Problem aside and set off toward the bus stop,
which was just outside the churchyard gate; she
was quite out of breath by the time she got
there and had to sit down for a while on the
waterproof seat of her walker. It was such a
handy gadget, not that she really needed such
a thing for the most part. It had been left
behind when herr Olsson, the civil engineer,
passed away. None of his children had bothered to collect it. They probably didn't even
know that the wheeled walker, which he had
kept just inside the door of the building,
belonged to their father. After his apartment
had been cleared and sold, it was still standing
there, and Maud had simply picked it up and
carried it into her own apartment. Last fall she
had twisted her knee when she tripped over a
rug and had reluctantly started to use the walker
when she had to go out shopping. The sidewalks
were very icy at the time, and she didn't want to
risk falling again. She quickly became aware of

its advantages: it provided useful support, she could sit on it and have a rest, she was suddenly offered a seat on the bus, people held the door open for her when she went into the stores, and middle-aged female shop assistants started treating her politely and . . . well, they really were quite sweet to her. The walker was a brilliant acquisition.

ONCE SHE WAS safely aboard the bus, her thoughts turned to Charlotte once more. Her sister had crept around their big, gloomy apartment like a restless soul, refusing to go out. Her mental state deteriorated rapidly during the 1960s. There was no point in suggesting that Maud might go away, even for one day. Her sister would go even crazier than she already was. Little Charlotte couldn't possibly manage all on her own! Who would cook her meals and make sure she took her medication? Who would be there when the fear dug its claws into her?

The worst thing was that it was all true. As Charlotte's illness gradually got worse, she needed stronger and stronger medication. She spent most of her time in a befuddled torpor. She should really have gone into an institution, but whenever her doctor suggested some kind of residential care, Charlotte always came to life and said sharply: "My sister would never allow such a thing! She and I have always lived together! She looks after me!"

Charlotte had been totally dependent on her sister for her daily care and survival. It didn't look as if Maud would ever have the opportunity to realize her own dreams.

At least not until the evening when Maud was standing in the kitchen, and suddenly felt a cold draft from the hallway. She hurried out to see what was going on and found the front door standing open. In her confused state, Charlotte had managed to unlock the door and had wandered out of the apartment. Maud sensed rather than saw her sister moving past the elevator door. There was a wide landing outside the elevator, with a staircase leading down to the main door of the apartment block. By the faint light seeping out from the elevator, Maud was just able to make out Charlotte's thin figure flitting anxiously to and fro. "Hello?" her voice echoed weakly. Slowly she moved closer to the edge of the landing. The stairs themselves were in total darkness. From Maud's point of view, it looked as if her sister was inching toward a black hole. The long, steep stone staircase . . .

The paralysis passed and she rushed toward the open door of the apartment. Charlotte was balancing on the top step. Maud had called out—or had she? She'd definitely tried to grab hold of her sister, hadn't she? She remembered feeling the slippery fabric of Charlotte's checked bathrobe against her fingertips, but her sister pulled away and then . . . disappeared . . . down into the depths of the darkness.

Three weeks later, Charlotte had passed away as a result of the severe concussion she had sustained. Maud spent every minute by her bedside. Her sister never regained consciousness. And that's when Maud's life had changed.

THE ICA GOURMET grocery store opened at nine o'clock in the morning on Christmas

Eve. Maud could see the manager unlocking the door as she stepped off the bus. She plodded over through the slush.

The manager waved to her. "Good morning! You're bright and early!" he called out cheerfully.

Maud smiled back at him. He was the person she spoke to more than anyone else these days.

"I thought I'd get my shopping done before all those stressed-out people start rushing around," she said.

"Very wise, very wise indeed," the manager said with a chuckle as he stacked boxes of raisins into a neat pyramid.

The little store had been there for as long as Maud could remember. To begin with it had sold only dairy products, but then it had expanded to become a minimart. Nowadays it was a gourmet grocery store, selling ready meals that could simply be heated up in the oven or microwave. They were prepared in a restaurant kitchen just a few miles away. The store also sold other delicious foods such as fine cheeses, exotic fruits, fresh bread baked on the premises, and all the other life essentials.

Maud placed two small cartons of rollmops in the basket of her wheeled walker, followed by a larger pack of herring salad. They were soon joined by a Stilton cheese in a blue porcelain pot, a mature Gorgonzola, a piece of ripe Brie, a packet of salted crackers, an artisan loaf that was still warm, a bunch of grapes, fresh dates, a jar of fig preserves, two bottles of julmust (the traditional Christmas soft drink), a small pack of new potatoes from the Canaries, a few clementines, and a box of After Eight chocolate mints. She was very pleased to find a portion of Jansson's Temptation in the prepared-foods section and quickly added it to her basket. Now there was only one thing missing from her Christmas table.

She pushed the walker over to the charcuterie counter. A young man who, in Maud's opinion, looked as if he was barely out of short pants was fiddling aimlessly with the prepackaged sausages on a shelf in front of the glass counter.

Maud stopped beside him and said, "I'd like a small, ready-cooked Christmas ham, please."

The young man pulled out one of his ear-buds. "What?"

Patiently Maud repeated what she had just said.

"Ready-cooked?" the boy echoed.

Maud nodded.

"I can, like, cut you some slices of that big one there. All the small ones are gone. There are so many old dudes living around here."

Maud thought his grin had something of a sneer about it. With considerable self-control, she nodded to indicate that she would like some slices of the ham behind the glass of the chill counter. As the boy walked past her he let out a loud yell that could be heard all over the store. The manager came rushing over from his pyramid of raisins, knocking the whole thing down in his panic.

"What's going on?" he wanted to know, sounding horrified.

"The old bat stabbed me!" the boy said, pointing an accusing finger at Maud.

She stooped over the handlebars of her walker. "What? What's he saying?" she said in a reedy voice.

The manager looked from Maud to the assistant, unsure what to do. "Go to the staff room and calm down!" he snapped at the boy.

"But the old bat—"

"Don't call the customer an old b . . . that word!" the manager growled, his face turning an alarming shade of bright red.

"What did he say?" Maud chipped in.

She was finding it difficult not to laugh. Carefully she closed the big safety pin and slipped it back into her pocket. She had thrust it into that unpleasant young man's buttock with all her strength. It was time someone taught him a lesson about old women! The pin was used to attach a reflective disc on a cord to the lining of her right-hand pocket, so she would be visible to motorists during the dark days of winter.

"Staff room, now!" the manager repeated in a tone that brooked no disagreement.

As the teenager shambled away, the

manager turned to Maud with a strained smile. "Please forgive the boy. He's only been here for a few days. He probably tripped and banged into a sharp corner. What can I get you?"

"I'd like four slices of your cooked ham. It's always so delicious," Maud replied, smiling sweetly.

SHE CARRIED THE wheeled walker up the wide stone staircase. There was no longer any sign of the bent little old lady who had been so bewildered by all the fuss in the grocery store not long ago. For someone who would be ninety in a few years, she was unusually strong.

A short while later, she was sitting in her favorite armchair with a steaming cup of coffee and a ham sandwich with plenty of mustard. The spiced rye bread flavored with wort smelled wonderful. She put on her glasses and began to read the morning paper.

That was when The Problem began to make its presence felt.

Maud looked at the clock. It was just before ten-thirty. That was unusually early for The

Problem. She sighed loudly and decided to try to ignore the whole thing for as long as possible. To her relief, The Problem stopped after a few minutes, and she was able to carry on with her reading.

AT AROUND TWO o'clock, Maud was woken from her afternoon nap. The Problem was in full swing. It seemed worse than ever. No matter how hard she tried, she couldn't ignore it.

The apartment building was five stories high and over a hundred years old. It was red brick built on a solid granite foundation. The ground floor housed a parking lot and a small number of shops. Despite the fact that Maud lived on the first floor, her window was almost fifteen feet above the ground. The walls were thick. The only weakness was the system of pipes throughout the building. If Maud was standing in the bathroom, she could hear almost every word from the neighbors on the floor above—particularly if they raised their voices.

And that was The Problem.

She couldn't pretend she didn't know about it, which was what she would have liked to do: avoid getting involved in The Problem. All she wanted was peace and quiet.

But The Problem couldn't be ignored. Maud couldn't shut out the sound of raised voices— mainly his voice—and the woman's sobbing. And the heavy thuds when he hit her and knocked her down. *Thump-thump-thud* was the sound that came through the ceiling of Maud's bedroom.

The Problem had begun the previous fall, when a famous attorney and his wife bought the apartment above Maud's. They were middle-aged and wealthy, and their children had already left home. According to the rumors, he had kicked up an enormous fuss when he wasn't allocated a parking space and had to put his name on a waiting list like all the other residents. He didn't like parking his flashy Mercedes on the street.

After renovations lasting several months, the attorney and his wife had moved in just before Christmas. *Peace at last*, Maud had thought. The construction noise had been unbearable.

Over the Christmas period exactly one year ago, Maud had realized that there was a big Problem. Christmas Eve was completely ruined, as far as she was concerned. The attorney had started abusing his wife in the afternoon, and it simply carried on. Maud had been unable to concentrate on the film starring Fred Astaire and Ginger Rogers on TV that night. All she could hear was quarreling and shouting from upstairs.

Early on December twenty-sixth, an ambulance turned up. Maud opened the door of her apartment just enough to hear the attorney's well-modulated voice.

"She fell down the stairs yesterday," he was saying to the paramedics. "I wanted to call you right away, but she didn't think it was anything serious. But when I saw how she looked today, I just had to call . . ."

Maud closed the door and screwed her face up in disgust. *Fell down the stairs! What a revolting man!* And he had ruined her Christmas.

After that, things were quiet for a few months. Twice during the spring she heard the attorney abusing his wife again. The week after Midsummer, Maud met the wife on the stairs. It was pouring outside, but the woman was wearing huge sunglasses. She had wound a big scarf around her head and pulled it well down over her forehead. Her entire face was covered with a thick layer of dark foundation. It didn't help. Maud could clearly see the eye that was swollen shut and the bruise like a purple half-moon over the cheekbone. They exchanged greetings, and the woman scurried past.

The charming attorney himself was a drinker. That was obvious to Maud whenever they passed on the stairs. He usually ignored her, but she couldn't miss the alcoholic fumes that lingered in his wake long after he had disappeared up the stairs to his apartment.

And now it was Christmas Eve once more, and The Problem was raising its ugly head again. Maud could hear the attorney's furious voice and his wife's sobs. *Thump-thump*, came the familiar sound from the floor above.

It was high time she did something about The Problem. Deep down, Maud had already made the decision before the idea began to form in her conscious mind. She went into the bathroom. The voices emerged clearly from the toilet bowl, and the ventilation duct amplified the sound.

"Fucking bitch! You useless fucking . . ."

Bang-bang-thud.

Maud clenched her fists in impotent fury. The anger that flared inside her made her heart beat faster.

"Sort out your face. You can't go out to the fucking parking meter looking like that," the attorney's voice echoed through the pipes.

Maud heard a sniveling mumble in response.

"I have to do everything myself . . . You are such a disgusting fucking mess . . . I'm going downstairs to get another pass. You can't even do that properly, you useless bitch! You were supposed to get a twenty-four-hour pass! What do you mean, you don't have any money? Don't you dare . . ."

Thump-thump.

Heavy footsteps crossed the floor above Maud's head, moving toward the hallway. She quickly hurried into her own hallway; cautiously she opened her front door and left it on the latch. She pushed the wheeled walker onto the landing and placed it next to the elevator. Anyone coming down the stairs on the other side wouldn't be able to see it, nor would anyone stepping out of the elevator. The stairwell was lit by a brass art nouveau-style lamp with a tulip-shaped glass shade. Without hesitation, Maud reached in and unscrewed the bulb. Now it wouldn't come on.

As she heard the door open on the floor above, she positioned herself behind the wheeled walker. She gripped the rubber handlebars firmly and waited.

Mumbling and muttering to himself, the attorney stumbled down the stairs. He was playing with the loose change in his coat pocket, trying to scoop it into his hand. He stopped right outside the elevator, fiddling with the coins. Maud could have reached out and touched his right shoulder. His boozy breath made her nostrils flare.

"Not enough cash . . . have to use my card . . . can't see a fucking thing . . ."

Swaying unsteadily, the attorney moved toward the wide marble staircase. Maud tensed her muscles. When he reached the edge of the top step, she summoned all her strength and shot across the landing, cannoning into his calves with the walker.

"What the f—"

That was all the attorney managed to say before he lost his balance and tumbled down the stairs, his arms waving helplessly. The dark, flapping overcoat made him look like a clumsy bat. Or possibly a vampire, Maud thought as she hurried back to her apartment. She did, however, remember to screw the bulb back in place before she went inside. She parked the wheeled walker just behind the door as usual. She didn't bother checking to see whether the attorney was still alive. The heavy thud when he hit the floor at the bottom of the staircase had sounded like a coconut being split open.

Only when Maud heard the sirens stop

wailing outside the main door of the apartment block did she open her own front door.

The neighbor opposite was standing in the stairwell, looking terribly upset.

"What's going on?" Maud asked, making an effort to appear slightly confused.

"Oh, I'm so glad you're home . . . I was just going to ring the bell . . . it's the lawyer . . . he's fallen down the stairs," the neighbor attempted to explain.

A young police officer came up and introduced himself to both women.

"Do you happen to know who the gentleman is?" he asked politely.

He was addressing the neighbor, who was at least twenty years younger than Maud. She told him the attorney's name and where he lived. The police officer nodded and said he would go and tell the man's wife what had happened.

"Those stairs are lethal. My sister fell down them," Maud said in a weak voice, pointing with a trembling finger. All at once the neighbor looked calmer.

"But Maud, my dear, that was before Gunnar and I moved in. And we've lived here for thirty-five years," she said, giving the police officer a meaningful glance.

She placed a protective arm around Maud's shoulders and steered her toward her apartment.

"Let's get you inside. You're very welcome to join us this evening if you like, but the children and grandchildren are coming over after they've watched Donald Duck on TV, so it might be a bit too noisy for you . . ."

The invitation remained hanging in the air, and Maud quickly grabbed hold of it. "No thank you," she said. "It's very kind of you, but . . . no thank you. I've got my television."

Behind her she heard one of the paramedics say to his colleague, "He stinks like a distillery."

THE AMBULANCE AND the police car had gone. Someone had come to collect the attorney's weeping wife.

Maud arranged all the goodies she had bought for her Christmas dinner on a tea cart.

She poured herself an ice-cold Aalborg Aquavit to go with the herring. It had been a stressful day, and she felt that she had earned a little drink. The delicious aroma of Jansson's Temptation was coming from the oven. Satisfied with the sight of the laden cart, she pushed it into the TV room and sank down into her armchair with a sigh of contentment.

At long last, the peace of Christmas descended on the old apartment block.

(2007)

I HAD RECENTLY retired and was strolling aimlessly around Stockholm one fine spring day, enjoying the sunshine. As usual I was without a companion. Walking alone was something I had grown accustomed to after losing my wife a couple of years earlier. In spite of my children and grandchildren, I sometimes felt a little lonely. After a few failed attempts at dating I had almost given up hope of finding a new partner, but suddenly there she was, in the middle of Stureplan. She stopped me as I was passing by.

"Excuse me, could you tell me where the Mushroom is?" she asked with a distinctive Gothenburg accent. She was so pretty, with her sparkling nut-brown eyes and curly blonde hair that at first I was completely tongue-tied. Eventually I managed to speak.

"If you turn around and look up, you'll see it."

She spun on her heel and gazed up at the concrete structure known as the Mushroom, for the simple reason that it looks exactly like one. Originally built to provide shelter from the rain for anyone waiting for a cab, the Mushroom became so well-known that people often arranged to meet there these days.

"Are you meeting someone?" I asked tentatively.

She broke into a dazzling smile. "Yes—you!"

Six months later we were married.

Mary is ten years younger than me, and back then she was still working as a cartographer for the highways department in Gothenburg. She had inherited a wonderful apartment in the city center from her parents—in Vasastan, to be exact. It's now been twenty-seven years since I moved in with her and became a citizen of Gothenburg.

I'M SURE YOU remember that June and July this year were rainy and pretty chilly, while August surprisingly turned into one long heat wave. Just as the warm weather arrived, our fine old apartment block was being cleaned. The housing association had decided it was time for the façade to have a much-needed facelift. The noise of the pressure washers started up at seven in the morning. The racket was enervating, and the protective sheet that hung over the building made the apartment quite dark. By the second week of the renovation project, we were heartily sick of the whole thing. Mary decided we should pack our swimming gear and a picnic lunch and take the number four streetcar out to Saltholmen. From there we usually hop on the first boat heading for one of the islands in the archipelago. It doesn't cost any more than an ordinary trip on the streetcar, and we retirees travel free on weekends and during the daytime from Monday to Friday.

We went down in the elevator, but when we came to step out, we could hardly get the door open. The entire landing and the staircase leading to the main entrance were crawling with police. The door of Maud's apartment was ajar, and I could see even more officers in the hallway.

What was going on? Had something happened to the old lady? Well, I say "old," but she's only a couple of years older than me, to be fair. My journalistic instincts from my days with the newspaper *Expressen* were aroused. Admittedly I spent most of my time reviewing various musical and cultural events, but I believe that any reporter worth his salt should have a nose for news. Besides which I used to supplement my meager salary by writing crime novels—not without a certain level of success.

Two uniformed officers were standing with their backs to us. Cautiously I tapped one of them, a young woman, on the shoulder. I noticed the thick braid hanging down her back; the rich, deep red color was strikingly beautiful.

"Excuse me. My name is Richard W. Bergh, author and journalist. My wife and I live on the top floor. What's happened? Is there anything I can do to help?"

She gave me a quick glance with her bright blue eyes, then ignored me. Undaunted, I asked my questions again, at which point her colleague turned around and looked down at me. To my surprise the tall officer was also a woman.

Before I had time to recover, she smiled and said, "Maybe you can help. Do you know everyone who lives in this section of the apartment block?"

"Yes, I've lived here for twenty-seven years."

She gazed at me searchingly, evaluating what she saw. I could tell that she was wondering whether it was worth bothering with what an old fool had to say.

In order to try to improve my standing, I quickly added, "During my career as a journalist in Stockholm, I often supported my good friend Detective Inspector Nils Thorén during homicide investigations. It's—"

"Never heard of him. Then again, I couldn't possibly know the name of every detective in Stockholm."

It was hardly surprising that the woman wasn't familiar with Nils Thorén, as my dear friend had retired at around the time she would have been starting elementary school.

"So you know everyone who lives in this section of the building, and now you're telling me you've been involved in homicide investigations," she went on. Her eyes narrowed. "In which case you'll be used to the sight of blood and dead bodies?"

"Oh yes, absolutely."

"Excellent. Come with me." Gripping my upper arm firmly, she led me toward the open door of Maud's apartment. Her colleagues moved aside to let us through, some of them giving me odd looks. I could see they were wondering why the old guy was heading for the crime scene.

The hallway was dark, but light was spilling out from two doorways. The first led to a kitchen where time had apparently stood still since the apartment block was built in 1918. The stove and the refrigerator had been replaced, but everything else bore a close resemblance to my parents' home on Tomtebogatan when I was a child. To be honest our kitchen was nowhere near as big, but the style and décor were the same.

It was fortunate that the policewoman had a firm hold on my arm because I caught my foot on something and almost tripped. It turned out to be a wheeled walker, parked underneath the hat shelf.

In the second room Maud was sitting in an armchair, sobbing quietly. I stopped and so did my escort. Maud is usually a very reserved person. She says hello to the neighbors and exchanges a few words about the weather, but she never engages in a longer conversation, nor does she socialize with any of us. I'm guessing this is because of the old feud about her apartment.

According to Mary, Maud had lived in the space rent-free for decades, to the dismay of the housing association and many of the tenants. I didn't blame her for taking advantage of her situation though. It was quite a good deal, and she was all alone, after all. Several different committees had tried to get rid of her over the years, but to no avail. Gunnar, who lives opposite her, once told me that she seemed to have plenty of money because she's away more than she's at home. And I do often see her coming and going with luggage.

Now, however, Maud was sitting in a small armchair in her combined living room and bedroom, sobbing away. Her hands were covering her face, and she seemed utterly devastated. A young police officer was perched on the bed next to her chair, clumsily patting her arm.

"I'll come and speak to her in a minute," my escort said.

Her colleague gave a start. "Okay, Inspector."

Inspector? The woman holding my arm was an inspector?

As if she'd read my mind, she said, "Detective Inspector Irene Huss. There's a dead man in this apartment; that poor lady found the body this morning. The smell led her to check out the rooms she doesn't normally use, and there he was."

With those words Detective Inspector Huss drew me back out into the hallway. I could understand why Maud had suspected that something was wrong; the farther we got, the stronger the repulsive stench became. We passed by several closed doors and through large rooms where the furniture was draped in white sheets; it was kind of spooky. The smell of death grew increasingly powerful, and in spite of the fact that I gave up smoking forty-two years ago, I desperately longed for a cigarette. Of course, I don't suppose the inspector would have let me light up. She kept going, still clutching my arm, seemingly impervious to the odor.

At long last we reached another open door, and I could see several figures dressed in white moving around inside the room. Detective Inspector Huss stopped.

"I'd like you to take a look at the victim to see if you recognize him. Is that okay?"

"Yes . . . yes, of course."

I found it quite difficult to answer because I was trying to hold my breath at the same time.

A forensic technician helped me put on paper overalls, shoe protectors, and a paper cap. To my eternal gratitude I was also given a mask to cover my mouth, although when I reached the doorway I realized it wasn't much help. Might as well get it over with. With the technician at my side, I stepped into the room.

It was like walking into a time capsule, a gentleman's room from a hundred years ago. Thick rugs, four generous brown leather easy chairs, somewhat the worse for wear, arranged around a low circular table with a copper top. A smoking table. My aunt, who had been married to a bank manager, used to have a similar one in her apartment on Strandvägen. There was a large display cabinet on one wall, with both glass doors wide open. Various silver objects were arranged on the shelves. My gaze fell on a painting next to the tiled stove, and for a few seconds I felt as if my heart was racing. Could it possibly be . . . ? I was jerked back to reality by the technician's voice in my ear.

"Don't go any farther; we don't want you stepping in the blood," he said quietly.

Bright lights on tripods illuminated the spot where the murder victim lay. There was absolutely no doubt that he'd been murdered. A considerable amount of dark, stinking blood had flowed out onto the floor, soaking into the Persian rug. Flies were buzzing around all over the place. The man was lying on his stomach in front of the tiled stove, and I could see a large bloody wound on the back of his head. Beside the body was a sturdy cast-iron poker. I noticed that he was wearing a smart dark-blue suit. The shirt cuffs poking out from his sleeves were pale pink, as was the sock that was just visible where one leg of his pants had ridden up. The soles of his shiny shoes were hardly scuffed at all. Evening wear. A strange choice during a heat wave, I thought, but what struck me as most odd were the white cotton gloves he was wearing. A short distance away from the body stood a large bag that appeared to contain something metallic that was catching the light.

The man's back was oddly humped, and it took a few seconds before I realized why. He had fallen head first, straight onto the decorative iron fender on the marble hearth in front of the stove doors. It was designed to look like the silhouette of a castle, and one of the turrets had gone straight through his right eye.

At that moment my head began to spin, and a wave of nausea flooded over me. The technician kindly led me out of the room to where the inspector was waiting. Together they sat me down on a chair and exhorted me to take deep breaths.

"Did you see anything you'd like to comment on?" Inspector Huss asked.

"Not . . . not really. He seemed to be very . . . blond," I managed to say. In spite of all the blood, I'd noticed a few fair curls at the back of his neck.

"Correct. Bleached hair, tied back in a ponytail. We'd put his age at between forty and fifty. Slightly overweight, medium height, well dressed in an evening suit and expensive shoes. Does that description fit anyone who lives in the neighborhood?"

It did, actually. But I couldn't understand what he was doing in Maud's apartment.

"He doesn't live in this block, but it could

be the man who's taken over the . . . the antique store in the building next-door."

To my annoyance my voice was less than steady, but the more I thought about it, the more certain I was that the victim was the antique dealer. What was his name again?

"What was his name?" the inspector asked, not surprisingly.

"I can't remember, but Mary—my wife— might know."

The technician helped me out of the protective clothing. The inspector took my arm once more, but this time I shook off her hand, politely but firmly. I no longer needed her support. We stopped outside the room where Maud was sitting, and to my surprise the inspector grabbed me again and steered me through the door.

"Your neighbor, Richard Bergh, has helped us with a possible identification of the victim; according to him, the deceased could be the man who runs the antique store next-door. Do you know him?" she asked in a pleasant tone of voice.

Poor Maud looked up at us, her eyes red and swollen with weeping, and shook her head. Inspector Huss turned to the young officer who was still at Maud's side and told him to go and find Mary and ask about the antique dealer's name. When he had disappeared, the inspector turned back to the shattered little figure in the armchair.

"Could you tell me your movements over the past week?" she said.

At first it seemed as if Maud hadn't realized that the question was directed at her, but just as the inspector was about to ask again, she answered in a reedy voice, "I . . . I've been away."

"For how long?"

"Four . . . no, five days."

"Where did you go?"

"Varberg. To the spa . . . Apelviken. I booked the trip on Monday morning when I was woken by a terrible racket outside—they're cleaning the building."

"But before that you were home?"

"Yes, but only for three nights. I arrived

back from Croatia last Friday. I spent a month there. But on Monday morning I was woken by a terrible . . ."

"I got that. So you were home for only three nights?"

"That's right, because on Monday morning I was woken by a terrible racket, so I booked a trip straight away . . . I went to Varberg . . . on the train. To the spa . . . what's it called? Oh yes, Apelviken. It's a spa."

The inspector gave a barely audible sigh, but then she smiled at Maud and continued in a friendly tone. "So did you take a walk around, check out the whole apartment when you got back from Croatia?"

"No, it was very late. And on Saturday I had to do my laundry, shop for groceries . . . on Sunday I went for a walk around town. It was such a beautiful day. I had lunch at a sidewalk café in Haga. I didn't think the work on the building would make such a noise, but on Monday morning I was woken by a terrible—"

This time the inspector interrupted her in what I felt was a rather abrupt manner.

"Yes, that kind of machinery does make a great deal of noise. So there was nothing to make you suspect that someone had been inside your apartment while you were away?"

Slowly Maud shook her snow-white head. Her hair was still surprisingly thick, and she always wore it in an old-fashioned chignon.

"No . . . I have three locks on the front door, and on the door leading to the cellar stairs. How . . . how did he get in?"

"One of the windows was ajar in the room where the body was found. Could you perhaps have opened it and forgotten to close it?"

At that Maud sat up straight, clearly offended. "Absolutely not! I haven't been in Father's room for four months!"

"And you're sure about that?"

"Indeed I am! I clean my room every week, along with the kitchen and bathroom. Then I tackle one or two of the other rooms each month. That's the only way . . . the only way I can manage . . ."

She fell silent and stared up at the inspector.

Her hands were shaking as she clasped them together on her lap.

"I might have . . . maybe I went in there and opened the . . . It was hot and stuffy when I arrived back from Croatia . . . But he can't have been lying there then, can he? I mean, surely I would have noticed? I don't remember if I went in and opened the window. Or did I do it before I went to Croatia? I don't remember!"

Her final words were a cry of despair. The outburst seemed to have used up the last of her strength; she slumped in her chair and sat there motionless, her head drooping.

A discreet cough came from behind us, and I turned to see the young police officer standing in the doorway. He looked pleased as he informed Inspector Huss that he had spoken to Mary.

"Fru Bergh says that the name of the man who took over the antique store three years ago is Frazzén. Double z. She didn't know his first name."

Without looking up, Maud asked in a weak,

broken voice, "What did he have . . . what was in the bag?"

"A pair of silver candelabra. Large and heavy. And a small silver goblet," Inspector Huss replied.

Maud nodded as if her suspicions had been confirmed. "The candelabra were a wedding present to my mother and father. They're always kept in the display cabinet in Father's room. We only get them out when we have a dinner party and set the table in the main dining room. Or rather . . . I mean . . . we used to . . ."

For a moment she looked completely confused, then she buried her face in her hands and began to sob once more.

Inspector Huss accompanied me to the door of Maud's apartment and thanked me for my cooperation.

I found Mary standing exactly where I'd left her.

"Maybe you don't want to go out to the islands after all this?" she said.

"I certainly do. I need to get that stench out

of my nose and take my mind off the whole thing," I said firmly.

Mary knew a little about Frazzén, the antique dealer. Apparently he specialized in gold and silver items. He had appeared on a TV program on several occasions, talking about and appraising objects that members of the public brought along.

THAT EVENING I called my good friend, the retired detective inspector Nils Thorén. He had just turned ninety-six. His body may be a little the worse for wear, but his mind is still crystal clear. I told him about the morning's upsetting events, taking care to make my account as accurate as possible. I also mentioned the painting I'd seen on the wall in the room where the body was found.

"Are you absolutely certain it's a genuine Anders Zorn?" he bellowed dubiously in my ear. Nils always shouts when he's on the telephone; his hearing isn't what it was. This doesn't bother me because I have a few problems in that department myself.

"Definitely. Art and jazz are my great passions, and I've written about both of them throughout my career as a journalist. The picture is a watercolor of two young and, naturally, naked young women bathing by the rocks. Not too large, around twenty-four by sixteen inches."

There was a lengthy pause.

"And what's it worth if it is genuine?" Nils asked eventually.

I took a deep breath before answering. "I've checked out the current market with Bukowskis, and a watercolor of that size would fetch between ten and thirteen million kronor."

The silence that followed was long and profound. Nils cleared his throat a couple of times before he spoke again.

"So all the doors were locked, with several locks in fact. There's scaffolding all around the building, covered with protective sheeting. And one of the windows in the room where the body was found was ajar. Which means the antique dealer got in via the scaffolding. The question is, how did he open the window? Most burglars would use a glass cutter, then reach in and undo the catch," he said.

"But Maud isn't sure whether she went in and opened the window after her month-long trip to Croatia. She was even babbling about the possibility that she might have done it before she went away. Which seems unlikely. We had a lot of rain in July, and I didn't notice any water damage to the parquet flooring under the window. It can't have been open for that long."

Another pensive silence.

"When did you say the scaffolding and the sheeting went up?"

"Almost two weeks ago."

"Which means the old lady must have opened the window when she arrived home after her long absence; an apartment soon begins to feel stuffy and oppressive during the summer months. So according to her, the man can't have been in the room at that point."

"No, but as I said, she seemed confused, and claimed that she couldn't really remember anything."

"Is she senile?" he asked sharply.

I thought carefully before I replied. "To tell the truth, I don't know her particularly well, but I've never seen any signs of what you might call dementia. She's always been able to take care of herself. And then there are those long trips she often takes . . . no, I wouldn't say she's ever seemed disorientated, not in the least. But maybe it was the shock?"

"Maybe. Did the forensic technicians find any indication that the antique dealer had an accomplice?"

I knew the answer to this because I'd heard them talking.

"Apparently they found the print of a man's shoe in the blood, but it was too indistinct to be of any use."

"How very convenient," Nils said dryly.

I realized he was thinking along the same lines as me.

"I'm guessing we're on the same page here," I said.

"It was the old lady who did it," he stated firmly.

"Yes, although I don't understand her motive. And why did she kill him in her own home? Plus how hard-bitten do you have to be to spend at least two nights in the same apartment as a corpse?"

"Or four."

"Four?"

"Yes. She arrived home from Croatia on Friday evening. If the murder took place then, we're looking at four nights. If the antique dealer was killed on Saturday, then it's three. And if it happened on Sunday, it's two. She didn't leave for Varberg until Monday morning. She got back after five days at the spa, then spent another night in the apartment before calling the police to say she'd found a dead body in her father's room. So that's between two and four nights in the same place as the deceased, in spite of the fact that she knew he was there the whole time. If this is true, she's one cold-blooded lady."

We both fell silent, going over the scenario in our minds. Was it really possible? But why would Maud . . . ? I could come up with only one explanation.

"I think she caught him stealing the silver and struck him with the poker. Maybe she didn't mean to kill him, but unfortunately he fell on the fender, and the sharp turret went straight into his eye and penetrated his brain. He died instantly. Maud decided to leave the candelabra and the cigar case in his bag. Perhaps she noticed that she'd stepped in the blood, so she dug out one of her father's shoes and pressed it down on top of her own print, making sure it was unusable."

"All very plausible, but nothing more than guesses and circumstantial evidence. We need to leave the investigation to Detective Inspector Huss and hope that the technicians find the evidence they need. These days there's DNA and all kinds of things that didn't exist back when I was working," Nils said.

"Okay, so we wait and see what happens," I agreed.

"I think that's for the best. I mean, we could be completely wrong. But, Richard, I wouldn't invite that old woman for tea anytime soon."

IT'S ALMOST CHRISTMAS now. Only yesterday I bumped into Maud on the stairs. She said hello as usual and kept on walking. I couldn't help shuddering from head to toe. That woman is lethal. The police still haven't solved the mystery of the antique dealer's murder. They're still looking for Frazzén's alleged accomplice, who left behind nothing but a blurred footprint. And a dead body.

No one has come up with a credible explanation, apart from Nils Thorén and me, but we can't prove anything. And what police officer would listen to a theory cooked up by two old men?

(2016)

AN

ELDERLY

LADY IS

FACED

WITH A

DIFFICULT

DILEMMA

M AUD HAD SPENT the whole day at airports and on board various planes. From Split in Croatia, with changes in Frankfurt and at Kastrup in Copenhagen, she had been traveling for almost nine hours. The advantage of the long journey was that it had given her time to think through a financial problem that had arisen.

The coffee and the meatball sandwich she had bought in the café at Landvetter had tasted good and had given her the strength to face the final leg of her trip on the airport bus into Gothenburg city center. As she got closer to home, she felt she was also getting closer to solving her problem.

When she arrived home, she dropped her suitcase and backpack on the floor in the hallway, then she walked resolutely to the other end of the apartment.

She had never even considered making any changes to the gentleman's room. It looked exactly as it had when her father passed away over seventy years ago. Sometimes when she stepped inside she thought she could detect a faint hint of cigar smoke still lingering in the air. That smell had never seemed so strong as it did right now.

She was dreading the difficult decision she had to make, but she knew it was high time to take a realistic view. She would soon be eighty-nine, and she had no heirs; when she was no longer around, everything would go to the state. And those vultures in the housing association would sink their talons into her lovely apartment. Carve it up into several smaller residences, carry out a "luxury" renovation and sell the properties at a high price. She had to accept that it was illogical to cling to objects for sentimental reasons. Over the years she had sold a number of paintings, including a Bruno Liljefors, a large Carl Larsson, and the modern piece by Nils Dardel. She had never liked the Dardel, but it had brought in the most money. She still had the Anders Zorn hanging on the wall in the gentleman's room. Around the turn of the previous century her father had traveled up to Dalarna himself and bought it from the artist. Mother found it offensive and always said she was glad it was in Father's room because that meant she didn't have to see it too often. Maud knew it was valuable, but she liked the image of the young women's bodies in the sunlight by the edge of the lake and didn't want to get rid of it yet.

She stood in front of her father's display cabinet for a while, lost in thought. The light from the crystal chandelier played on the shining surfaces of his silver collection. Before Christmas every year she polished each item, which took at least three days. She could make better use of that time. She could go traveling, for example, but that was expensive. She knew the objects behind the glass doors were worth a great deal. She needed money. Lots of money. The situation wasn't exactly critical, but she'd decided on a vacation that would make a significant hole in her finances.

She wanted to go on a real top-notch trip to South Africa, something she'd been dreaming of for years. Admittedly she'd already been there twice, but on those occasions she had stayed in simple but clean hotels, as usual, and had traveled from place to place by bus and train. But the distances between the sights were considerable, which meant she hadn't seen even a fraction of what she'd had in mind.

Now she was planning a proper tour with a Swedish-speaking guide. Five-star hotels. An exclusive lodge in the Kruger National Park while on a safari; she hoped to see the "big five": lions, elephants, rhinos, leopards, and buffalo. And she was also scheduling outings to vineyards, fantastic dinners at the best restaurants, a visit to Victoria Falls, a cruise along the Zambezi River, and a week in Cape Town. It would be twenty-four days in total and luxury all the way. Her last hurrah.

It would cost an arm and a leg. But what the

hell? She might as well make her dream a reality before she got too old, because to be perfectly honest, she could no longer cope with dragging her suitcases around and using public transportation in the suffocating heat. Or sitting on a bus that had gotten stuck in a muddy ditch after a cloudburst, which had happened to her more than once. Above all, it took too long. Traveling around Europe is one thing, but Africa isn't as safe for an elderly lady. The years were passing by, and she wasn't getting any younger. She was still fit and healthy, and a trip like this wouldn't be a problem. She had never chosen the deluxe option before, but right now it seemed like an excellent choice for . . . yes, an elderly lady. And she would escape Christmas and New Year's in Sweden. It would be high summer in South Africa then. However, there were only twenty-two spots available; she would need to book it in the very near future.

The silver collection just had to go.

It was the antique dealer who'd taken over for old Helmut Goldman who'd made her even consider taking such a step. The young man was called Frazzén, of all the ridiculous names. A real popinjay, who wore his over-long hair in a silly ponytail.

One mitigating circumstance was of course the TV program *Antiques Roadshow*. It was one of Maud's favorites and had been running for several seasons. Frazzén was one of the appraisal experts, specializing in gold and silver. She had to admit that he'd made a good impression; he seemed trustworthy, and he certainly knew what he was talking about. The fact that the store was just next door had decided the matter; she would sell the collection to Frazzén the popinjay.

It was already five forty-five, and he closed at six. Carefully she picked up a little silver goblet from the top shelf. Father had often pointed to it and told her that the smallest item was in fact the most valuable. She knew it dated from the seventeenth century and thought it had belonged to some French king.

Something told her that Frazzén would take the bait.

THE STREET WAS deserted, and only a few cars were parked in the designated spaces. The air was shimmering over the warm tarmac when Maud stepped out of the front door of the apartment block. It was like walking into a sauna, but she was used to the heat. In her blue summer dress and a thin cotton cardigan, she felt cool. She was wearing white sandals and carrying a pale-beige purse. She saw Frazzén emerge through the glass door of his shop, engraved with the words: GOLDMAN'S ANTIQUES, EST. 1950, SUCCESSOR W. FRAZZÉN, EXPERT IN GOLD & SILVER. The antique dealer was kitted out in a dark-blue suit and pink shirt and looked as if he was going straight from work to some kind of dinner dance. *Impractical and too warm in this weather*, Maud thought.

She reached him just as he turned the key in the last security lock. He gave no indication that he'd seen her as he pulled down a heavy metal grate that covered both the door and the shop window. Then he pressed a little round object attached to his key ring, and Maud heard a loud beep. The lock responded with an audible click, confirming that the store was well and truly closed for the day.

He then turned to Maud and quickly looked her up and down.

"Electronic lock," he informed her, nodding in the direction of the grate.

"Very practical. I gather you're closed for the weekend," Maud said.

"Absolutely—in fact I'm on vacation for the next three weeks," Frazzén replied, favoring her with a dazzling white smile.

Those veneers must have cost you a fortune, she thought, pursing her lips, but of course she didn't say it out loud.

"I believe you're an expert on precious metals, herr Frazzén," she began as she fumbled with her purse zipper, which had caught on the fabric. When she eventually managed to get it open, she reached in and brought out a small item wrapped in newspaper. Frazzén's expression was skeptical as she produced the little silver goblet, but his eyes widened when he saw the beautifully decorated artifact with its gilded interior. His hand trembled as he took it from her. He reached into his inside pocket and took out a small case containing an eyeglass. He brought it up to his eye and examined the mark on the base of the goblet.

"Excellent . . . excellent. French . . . royal provenance," he murmured to himself. Reluctantly he handed the goblet back to Maud and fired off another blinding smile.

"Did you want this appraised, or are you hoping to sell it?"

"Sell. And there's more."

Maud explained her father's predilection for antique silver and said she had decided to sell the lot. Frazzén didn't even try to hide his interest in seeing the entire collection. Unfortunately he didn't have time to pop up to Maud's apartment at the moment.

"A few of us are having a kind of memorial celebration for a friend who died recently. He lives—lived—in Australia, so none of us were able to get to the funeral."

That explained the dark suit, but was it

really necessary to wear something like that when the weather was so warm? Maybe so, if it was a memorial, Maud thought. She decided not to get hung up about his clothes.

"And as I said, I'm away for three weeks from tomorrow; I'm driving down through Europe then on to England on a combined vacation and business trip," Frazzén added.

Maud thought fast. "Will it go on until late? The memorial, I mean."

"No, we'll be finished just after eight. The other guys are involved in a yacht race in Marstrand tomorrow; they have an early start, so they need to get a good night's sleep."

"Is there any chance you might be able to come around after the memorial?" she asked.

Frazzén didn't even think about his response. "I'll be there by nine at the latest," he said immediately, with yet another beaming smile. Even if that smile was heartfelt, there wasn't the slightest hint of warmth in his eyes; Maud saw only cold calculation. That little goblet had aroused his greed. *Good*, she thought. *It's going to cost you.*

THE DOORBELL RANG at precisely nine o'clock, and Maud let Frazzén in. He had obviously come straight from the memorial because he was still wearing the dark-blue suit. His limp handshake was warm and damp, like a wet dishcloth, and he was surrounded by an unpleasant miasma of men's fragrance and sweat.

"I brought this along—I just happened to have it in the car," he said, holding up an oversized bag.

That wasn't quite what Maud had been expecting. She'd thought he would simply give her an appraisal that evening; she had no intention of handing over the collection until she'd received the money. A seed of suspicion began to grow inside her. How serious was this guy? She remembered how those cold, calculating eyes had fastened on the silver goblet. How reluctant he had been to hand it back to her. She was going to have to watch him, even if he was a TV star. Or maybe for that very reason.

Without a word Maud turned on her heel

and indicated that he should follow her. In her peripheral vision she could see Frazzén's head moving from side to side as he tried to take in all the antiques they passed on the way to the gentleman's room. She could almost hear the calculator clicking away inside his brain. Most of the furniture was draped in white sheets, but he could see the paintings and some of the ornaments.

The room lay in darkness because the apartment block was undergoing a facelift. It was surrounded by scaffolding and enveloped in a protective sheet that blocked the natural light. Maud went in and switched on the light. Frazzén stopped in the doorway and gazed around. Then he looked at her, flashing those goddamn veneers.

"Fantastic! A room that hasn't been touched for a hundred years!" he exclaimed with delight.

Maud simply nodded. It was true, she thought, time had stood still in this room.

The antiques expert strode over to the display cabinet. He couldn't suppress a gasp, but

when he turned to Maud, his face registered
nothing more than polite interest.

"This looks quite promising, but it might
take me a while to go through everything.
Could I possibly have a glass of water? Or a coffee, if you don't mind?"

She'd had no intention of offering him anything, but it had been a very warm day, and he
was bound to be thirsty.

"I'm out of coffee. I only got home this afternoon after a month overseas, and I haven't had
time to go shopping. I'd be happy to fetch you
some water, if that's okay."

"That would be wonderful!"

Maud headed for the kitchen, leaving the
door of Father's room ajar. It was a trick she'd
learned as a child. When the gentlemen were
sitting in there bragging over a glass of
whisky and smoking fine cigars, she would
creep up and peep in through the gap by the
hinges. She had heard many scabrous tales
that way, and no one had ever caught her.

She crossed the dark parquet floor of the
salon, making as much noise as possible with

the heels of her slippers. When she reached the other side of the room, she quickly slipped them off and crept back, keeping as close to the wall as possible because the floor didn't creak there.

When she peered through the gap, her suspicions were confirmed.

Frazzén had taken out the impressive candelabra adorned with crystal prisms, along with the little seventeenth-century silver goblet, and placed them on the smoking table. But he was no longer examining them; instead he was standing in front of the Zorn painting. He glanced over his shoulder toward the door. Maud held her breath and didn't move a muscle. Once Frazzén had reassured himself that he was alone, he turned his attention to the picture once more.

Maud felt a surge of ice-cold fury. That revolting man was planning to swindle her. As if it wasn't enough that he was clearly set on taking the most valuable silver pieces with him today, he was also intending to steal the Zorn.

Slowly she slithered backward in her

stocking feet. Behind her was a large tiled stove that used to heat the salon, and beside it stood a heavy gilded bronze companion set consisting of a poker and a small brush and shovel for clearing out the ashes. Silently she unhooked the poker and shuffled back to the door.

Frazzén was just reaching up to take down the painting when Maud made her move.

She had played tennis for many years and had been given lessons by skilled coaches. She had given it up at least twenty years ago, but the muscle memory was still there. She executed a perfect backhand, striking the thieving bastard on the back of the head. He never knew what had happened; he simply went down without uttering a sound. There was an unpleasant crunch as he hit the floor, and a pool of blood immediately began to form. Oddly enough, the wound Maud had inflicted wasn't bleeding nearly enough to explain the quantity appearing under Frazzén's head. She edged closer and saw that he had landed on the decorative fender, and one of the sharp, pointed turrets had gone straight into his eye.

He was as dead as a doornail, and Maud realized she was now faced with a rather difficult dilemma.

She stood there motionless for a long time, assessing the scene. There was no way she could move the dead man. For one thing he was too heavy, and for another he was impaled on the fender. He would just have to stay where he was.

She wouldn't touch him, but she would make various adjustments to the room.

First of all, however, she needed to work out a plan. Time to dig out the coffee she'd bought at the airport.

On the way back to the kitchen she became aware that she was still clutching the bronze poker. It would have to be meticulously cleaned, until not the slightest trace of blood remained. Then it must disappear forever.

MAUD WAS NESTLED deep in her favorite armchair, sipping a cup of coffee. On the table beside her was a plate with a half-eaten egg sandwich. It was going to be a long night; she needed an energy boost. She had gone through various scenarios and had settled on a strategy. It was watertight; she had no intention of ending her life in jail.

Resolutely she stood up and went into the kitchen. She got out a pair of brand-new rubber gloves, put them on, and headed for the bathroom. The bronze poker lay in the tub in a strong chlorine solution. She let out the water, picked up the poker and dried it with a clean towel, which she then wrapped around the murder weapon. She took it into the hallway and removed the spare key from the cupboard next to the front door. She opened the door cautiously and peered out into the silent stairwell. Not a sound from her neighbors. Most of them were probably still away on vacation, and if they were back at work, they were no doubt spending the warm weekend out in the country or on a boat.

With the poker in one gloved hand and a flashlight in the other, Maud stepped out onto the landing. Guided by the light shining through the small window in the elevator door, she began to make way to the cellar stairs. She had lived in this building all her life; she knew every step, every passageway. However, she moved with extreme caution; it would be a disaster if she fell and broke her leg or her foot. Only when she had almost reached the cellar door did she dare to switch on the flashlight.

With a screech from its rusty hinges the door leading to the storage compartments slowly opened. Maud pressed the button just inside and the bare bulbs dangling from the ceiling came on, which meant she no longer needed the flashlight. She marched over to her compartment, which was the largest of them all—another thorn in the side of the housing association. They didn't think a single elderly lady should have such a privilege, but as far as Maud was concerned, it made perfect sense; she needed the space. It was absolutely full, and with the best will in the world, it would be nearly impossible to fit in anything bigger than a sheet of tissue paper. However, Maud knew exactly what she was looking for, and she also knew exactly where everything was.

After moving various boxes and pieces of furniture, she managed to reach her father's old golf bag. First of all she pushed the towel right to the bottom of the bag, followed by the poker. She removed the protective leather cover from one of the clubs and slipped it over the section of the poker that was protruding from the bag. The leather was dry and cracked with age, but it had retained its shape. Nobody would suspect it was concealing anything other than a golf club.

Quickly Maud pushed her way through to a wooden chest by the wall. It wasn't locked, and when she opened the lid, her nostrils were assailed by the smell of mothballs. The chest contained men's clothes, along with several pairs of shoes. Her father had been something of a snob when it came to his attire, and he had taken very good care of his footwear. Over the years he'd grown quite stout, but he hadn't been particularly tall. He'd had small feet for a man: size 41. She knew precisely what she was looking for—there they were, the light summer shoes. They'd hardly been worn, and still looked new. A triumphant smile crossed her narrow lips as she took the shoes out of their protective silk bag. They were just the thing: perforated light-brown leather, with smooth soles.

She checked out a couple of nearby boxes and eventually found the "Left Behind" box. In it were all the items her various tenants had left behind. The last one had moved out twenty-five years ago, but she hadn't been able to bring herself to throw anything away. She had placed the articles of clothing in large plastic bags and remembered seeing a black, long-sleeved T-shirt and a pair of scruffy blue jeans. They'd been left by Martin, who was an unbearable young man. She'd thrown him out after he had come home rolling drunk late one night. She had made it very clear to her tenants that there was to be no alcohol and no smoking. And Martin had been a theology student! After she'd bawled him out, he'd stormed off without taking anything with him and had never come back. His clothes would be very useful now; he'd been quite slender, and she thought they would fit her pretty well.

Satisfied with her raid on the cellar, she made her way back up the stairs.

As THE CLOCK on Vasa Church struck one, Maud crept out through the door from the inner courtyard. This was the darkest time of the night, which was important. No one must see her in the long-sleeved T-shirt, the jeans, and her father's shoes. Her white hair was hidden beneath a tightly knotted dark blue scarf, and she had swapped the rubber gloves for a thin leather pair. The door led out to a side street. She knew both windows of the gentleman's room overlooked it. The city's nightlife was in full swing just a few hundred yards away, with people talking and laughing, streetcars screeching, and vehicles hooting, but there wasn't a soul in sight in the alley. She closed the door with great care, and made her way along by the wall. After a few steps she reached the scaffolding. Without hesitation she began to climb. It was a little difficult to pull herself up onto the planks, but she managed. It was quite dark because of the protective sheeting, and she felt her way along before each step. She passed one window, but because it belonged to her salon, there was nothing to worry about. The next was the gentleman's room, and she had opened it a fraction before setting off on her nocturnal adventure. She pushed it wider and climbed into the room. Without even glancing at the body by the stove, she crossed the floor and walked all the way through the apartment to the front door. She took the spare keys out of the cupboard and unlocked all three locks. She grabbed the handle, but didn't open the door. Then she locked up again and replaced the keys before returning to the gentleman's room.

She switched on the main light so that she could see properly. There was no risk of anyone looking in, thanks to the protective sheeting outside. She mustn't tread in the blood—not yet. She moved around to the smoking table, picked up both candelabra and the silver goblet, and placed them in Frazzén's oversized bag, which was on the floor. She left it unzipped so that the silver artifacts were clearly visible.

She circled around the pool of blood until she could reach the cast iron companion set, which in this case consisted of a poker, tongs, and a small shovel. She grabbed the poker, considered the distance and angle, and with all her strength she brought it down on the already significant wound in the back of the antique dealer's head. It was essential that the pattern match the murder weapon. Both pokers appeared to be the same size, but one could never tell. Best to make absolutely certain.

Satisfied with the result, Maud dropped the poker next to the body. Then she placed one foot in the edge of the pool of blood, deliberately sliding her shoe back and forth in order to blur the impression. She switched off the light, went back to the window and climbed out onto the scaffolding, leaving small bloodstains on the sill and the wooden planks.

When she reached the ground she took a few steps out into the street and walked around a parked car. She stopped by the driver's door before taking one big stride backward into the middle of the road. She bent down, quickly removed her father's shoes and slipped them in the plastic bag she'd brought along in the pocket of her jeans.

Frazzén's accomplice had left his trail.

And now that trail had come to an abrupt end.

She tiptoed back to the door in her thick socks.

MAUD HAD BEEN in a deep, dreamless sleep for five hours when the alarm clock went off. The tension had eased once she'd formulated a plan, which seemed to have worked well so far. All she had to do now was carry it through to the end.

After her usual breakfast of egg, a cheese sandwich, and several cups of strong coffee, she began to deal systematically with anything that could possibly lead to her. She washed the clothes she'd been wearing the previous night on the machine's hottest program. There had been no sign of blood on them, but one could never be sure. Two hours at ninety degrees should remove most traces. Meanwhile she cleaned the shoes meticulously with a strong chlorine solution. It broke her heart to treat Father's fine summer shoes so harshly, but it was all for a good cause. She threw the thin leather gloves, the rubber gloves, and her thick socks in the trash; the garbage was due to be collected on Monday morning.

When the washing cycle finished, she hung the clothes on the line above the bathtub, then she did another load: sheets and towels at sixty degrees. Finally she filled the drum with her laundry from Croatia. That should ensure that there were absolutely no traces of blood in the machine.

She decided it was time for lunch. She poured herself a glass of beer, ice-cold from the refrigerator. She made a couple of cheese sandwiches; she wasn't very hungry in this heat. She placed everything on a tray and carried it out onto the balcony overlooking the courtyard. It was pleasantly cool in the shade, and she allowed herself to enjoy her meal and the peace and quiet.

She spent the afternoon cleaning the kitchen, the bathroom, and her combined bedroom and living room. It was another hot day, and she had no desire to go out; however, she realized she needed to shop for food. Everything must appear normal, even if there weren't many people around right now.

At about six o'clock she set off with her wheeled walker. In the basket was a tightly knotted trash bag, which she dropped in one of the dumpsters in the courtyard. This time there was no need for her to sneak surreptitiously through the door leading to the street. She ambled slowly along to the Hemköp store on Vasagatan, where she purchased a six-pack of Carlsberg, some fruit and vegetables, potato salad, ice cream, and a roast chicken, which would last her for two days. She had no intention of staying home any longer than that. She had already bought coffee, milk, eggs, and cheese at the airport the previous day.

Later she enjoyed a delicious chicken salad on the balcony. She treated herself to a glass of port to accompany the ice cream, and she topped it off with a cup of coffee. If it hadn't been for the dead body in the gentleman's room, it would have been the perfect conclusion to a lovely summer's day.

AT SEVEN O'CLOCK on Sunday morning Maud was ready to travel the short distance to Järntorget by streetcar. She had put the clothes and shoes from Friday night in a large paper carrier, and she had also added some of Charlotte's clothes and shoes, which had been kept in her sister's dressing room since her death. Maud knew she should have given everything away long ago, but somehow she hadn't been able to face the task.

The bag was in the basket of her wheeled walker. She made her way to the stop, which was no more than a hundred yards from her door. When the streetcar arrived she clambered aboard, and traveled two stops. As a retiree, she didn't have to pay. She got off at Järntorget and took a moment to assess the situation.

The air was still cool at this early hour, but the sun was shining in a cloudless sky. It was going to be at least as hot as yesterday. There were few people around in the large, open square at this time on a Sunday, just the odd passenger, presumably planning to travel out to Saltholmen. From there they could hop aboard one of the boats heading out into the archipelago. An elderly man was sleeping outside a sidewalk café, using a large backpack as a pillow. Judging by his torn, dirty clothing he was a rough sleeper. It was a shame he was so tall, otherwise Maud could have placed her paper carrier next to him.

Slowly she set off in the direction of the Rosenlund Canal. In order to make herself look a little shorter and older, she stooped over her walker. She had pulled on a white fabric sunhat with a wide brim, which hid her hair and part of her face. No one took any notice of the elderly lady. She crossed Vasagatan and continued to the Salvation Army's secondhand store. Maud had always wondered why they called their stores *Myrorna*—"the Ants."

Maybe because they saw themselves as busy little ants, working hard in the service of the Lord? Not that it mattered; the important thing was that they accepted clothes and other items which they sold or passed on to those in need. As she walked by she paused and left the paper carrier by the door. They could do whatever they wanted with the contents; there was no way any of those clothes or shoes could be connected to her. With the same shuffling gait she slowly returned to the streetcar stop and went home.

She spent the rest of the day in town, with neither sunhat nor wheeled walker. She had a most enjoyable lunch at a sidewalk café in Haga. To be honest, the whole area was a gigantic tourist trap, but she still found it charming. The best thing was that none of the people bustling along took any notice of her. An elderly lady out and about in the lovely weather didn't attract much attention.

Maud had been in town, behaving exactly as she always did.

WHEN SHE WAS woken at seven on Monday morning by the noise of the pressure washers cleaning the outside of the apartment block, she smiled to herself before swinging her legs over the side of the bed. She picked up her cell phone and pressed a pre-programmed number. A young female voice answered, and Maud did her best to sound old and a little shaky.

"Hello? Hello? Is that Apelviken Spa? Good, good. I was wondering if you might have a single room free from today until Friday. That's right, five days. You do? Marvelous, I'll take it! Full board, please!"

She ended the call and switched on her laptop. First of all she booked a round-trip ticket to Varberg on the train departing from Gothenburg's central station at lunchtime. There was one more thing she needed to do online. With the help of Google, she soon found what she was looking for: discreet hearing aids. She ordered two.

SHE HAD SPENT five wonderful days by the sea. Her room had a view over the Kattegat, the weather had been beautiful, and the food particularly delicious. Her spa break couldn't have been better.

Maud was feeling very pleased with herself as she unlocked the door of her apartment on Friday evening. As soon as she stepped inside she became aware of an unpleasant odor that wasn't usually there. Since she knew where it was coming from, she ignored it. She unpacked, put her dirty laundry in the washing machine and switched it on. Then she went for a walk in the warm summer's evening. By the time she got back it was almost eight o'clock, and the laundry cycle had finished. She hung up her washing, then went into the kitchen and made herself two cheese sandwiches. She took a beer out of the refrigerator but didn't bother pouring it into a glass. Before switching on the TV, she checked that the door to the hallway was firmly closed, and just to be sure she wouldn't have to deal with that bothersome smell, she opened the window. She sank down in her armchair with a contented sigh. TV2 was showing Hitchcock's *The Birds* from 1963. It was one of her favorite movies—creepy, but very good.

AFTER HER USUAL breakfast on Saturday morning, Maud decided it was time. She took a deep breath before going into the hallway and setting off through the apartment. The closer she got to the gentleman's room, the more unbearable the repulsive stench became. She hesitated for a fraction of a second, then opened the door and glanced in the direction of the tiled stove. Everything was exactly the same as it had been a week ago, apart from the flies and the smell. In order to reinforce the impression that she'd had a shock, she didn't close the door completely. Without hurrying, she went into her bedroom, picked up her cell phone and called the emergency number. When a female voice answered, Maud began to whimper and stammer:

"He's . . . he's dead . . . there's such a terrible smell . . . police please . . . could someone come? You have to come! He's . . . he's just lying there, in Father's room! And he's DEAD! Please help me, I don't know what to do!"

After a little while the woman on the other end managed to extract Maud's details.

"Stay in your bedroom until the police arrive and ring your doorbell," she advised.

"I will . . . I promise. But please come quickly!" Maud sobbed.

She ended the call with a grim smile on her thin lips.

RAIN WAS PATTERING gently against the windows. Dark clouds hung low over the city, enveloping the whole place in miserable, gray dampness. Fall was approaching implacably. The lights were on in the conference room, where the investigation team had gathered to review "the mystery of the murdered celebrity antique dealer," as the media had dubbed the case.

Detective Inspector Embla Nyström was feeling frustrated. Frazzén had been killed almost four weeks ago, and they had gotten precisely nowhere.

"Okay, let's go through everything we know; surely we can solve this," her boss, Superintendent Tommy Persson, said briskly.

None of his colleagues appeared to be enthused by his tone of voice. They all recognized the signs of an investigation that was going nowhere. Tommy had his laptop open in front of him, sending images to the screen. Right now he was showing a close-up of the wound on the back of Frazzén's head.

"The victim suffered a blunt force trauma to the upper section of the base of the skull —two powerful blows, in fact, inflicted with a cast iron poker. Forensics confirmed this was the weapon."

He switched to a photograph of the poker lying in a pool of blood.

"The blows could definitely have killed Frazzén, but the actual cause of death was the sharp turret on the decorative fender, which penetrated his eye and his brain when he fell onto it."

The next image was of the turret, buried

deep in the eye. Embla had become hardened
to gruesome sights during the two years she'd
spent with the Violent Crimes Unit, but this
made her feel sick. No one could be unmoved
by such horror.

"We've established that the murder took
place on Friday, August tenth. Frazzén spent
some time with friends at a memorial celebration that evening, and they've confirmed that
he was wearing the same clothes. The forensic
pathologist is also satisfied that this date fits in
with his observations. The victim was discovered on Saturday, August eighteenth. Because
of the heat and the flies, the body deteriorated
significantly during the period when it lay
undiscovered. We had record temperatures
that week, if you recall."

Tommy clicked on the next picture.

"The impression of a shoe in the blood. It's
not at all clear, and only the front part of the
sole is visible; we didn't manage to find a print
of the heel. However, forensics say it's a size
forty-one. The sole is smooth, probably made
of leather—as was the case with the victim's

shoes, but his were size forty-four. We suspected that one of his friends from the memorial might have acted as his accomplice, but they've provided one another with an alibi for the whole evening and night. After the gathering they all traveled to Marstand together and spent the night in a summer cottage. They had to be up early to take part in a twenty-four-hour yachting race."

Tommy then moved on to images of small bloodstains on the windowsill and a few faint marks on the planks outside the window.

"The accomplice climbed out of the window and probably took off in a car that was parked directly below," he said.

"And that's where the trail ends," Embla muttered out of the corner of her mouth to Detective Inspector Irene Huss, who was sitting next to her.

Tommy stared at her, and she realized he'd heard her comment. Eventually he looked away and pointed to the bloodstains.

"That's where the trail ends because we have no idea who was with Frazzén. We've established that it was his accomplice who climbed up the scaffolding. Presumably the old lady who lives in the apartment had left the window ajar herself because there's no sign of a break-in. She's more than a little confused. So the guy simply jumped inside, walked to the front door and let Frazzén in. Forensics found traces of dust from the planks throughout the apartment. The keys were in a cupboard by the door. Together they went back to the room containing the silver, and something happened. They had an argument for some reason, and the accomplice hit the antique dealer on the back of the head with the poker. It's worth noting that there were no signs of a struggle in the room. The victim must have turned his back on his companion, who attacked him from behind before making his escape through the window."

Irene Huss raised her hand, and Tommy Persson gave her a nod.

"So why didn't this guy take anything with him when he ran away? The silver goblet is small enough to slip in his pocket."

"Panic," Tommy said curtly.

No doubt that was the most-likely explanation, but Embla wasn't convinced. Something didn't feel right, although she couldn't quite put her finger on what it was.

Tommy stretched and gazed at his team. "Anyway, now we know how Frazzén found out about the silver collection, and where it was kept."

One corner of his mouth twitched into a half-smile when he saw the effect of his words. This had been a mystery from the start: How could the antique dealer have known about the collection?

He had everyone's undivided attention as he continued. "The old lady called me late yesterday afternoon. She said she's starting to get over the worst of the shock, and she suddenly remembered something. When she got home from her overseas trip on the Friday, she bumped into Frazzén outside his store; he was just closing up for the day. She recognized him from that antiques show on TV and started talking to him. She's pretty sure she mentioned some of the silver artifacts, and that they were in a display cabinet in her father's room. Frazzén offered to come up and give an appraisal, but he said it would have to be when he returned from his vacation. She's not quite all there, little Maud, but this conversation has come back to her. Which explains a great deal."

Indeed. Although clearly the antique dealer had had no intention of waiting until after his vacation; he wanted to fit in the home visit before he left. Without paying for anything he liked the look of.

"Was it because he was going away on vacation that it took so long for Frazzén to be reported missing?" asked Inspector Hannu Rauhala.

"Yes. According to his sister, he was planning to drive down to Calais, then take the ferry over to England. He didn't usually call her for several days when he was traveling, but when she hadn't heard from him for a week and couldn't get a hold of him on his cell phone, she started to worry, and contacted the police. The following day he was found dead by little Maud," Tommy confirmed.

So Maud found him in her apartment . . . Embla was thinking hard. "But surely she must have been sleeping in the apartment on the night when Frazzén was killed," she said. "Didn't she hear anything?"

Tommy frowned, and Embla realized she hadn't requested permission to speak.

"Of course I asked her that very question, but she said she was completely exhausted after her journey home from Croatia and went to bed early—around nine-thirty, she thought. And she has hearing problems. She wears hearing aids in both ears, and takes them out at night. Plus she always closes the bedroom door, and she'd taken a sleeping tablet. So she was dead to the world, as she put it."

Embla had thought that old people were light sleepers, but Maud's explanation sounded convincing. Very convenient for the intruders.

"Do we have any information about the guy who was with Frazzén?" she asked, after obediently waving her hand.

Tommy spread his hands apologetically. "No. All we know is that he's probably slightly below average height, shoe size forty-one. We didn't find any fingerprints or DNA. He was wearing gloves."

Embla's hand shot up again. "What traces did forensics find?"

"As I said, all the killer left behind was that blurred half-footprint in the blood, plus a few minor stains on his way out. A lot of the fingerprints could be ruled out because they were too old. The freshest we found belonged to Maud herself—none from Frazzén, because he was wearing cotton gloves. However, he did provide us with a hell of a lot of DNA."

His colleagues smiled as he delivered the understatement of the day.

"No prints on the poker?" Embla persisted, ignoring the dig.

"No—only old blurred ones. Nothing new."

Tommy looked down at his notes before continuing. "As you're already aware, Frazzén was openly gay; it was no secret. However, according to his sister he wasn't in a long-term relationship at the time of his death, and the friends he met at the memorial confirmed that."

Embla's hand was up again. "Would he really take a new boyfriend along if he was breaking into someone's apartment?"

"We don't know. And they weren't necessarily a couple, just partners in crime."

A couple of people smiled dutifully, but Embla hadn't finished.

"It bothers me that this guy was able to get in through an open window. Don't you think it's a little too convenient? The fact that it was open and couldn't be seen from the street. And we checked: the scaffolding and the sheeting completely hid the window."

She looked to Irene for confirmation, and Irene nodded. Tommy shrugged.

"Maybe he just got lucky. If the window hadn't been ajar he probably would have used a glass cutter and opened the catch. It wouldn't have taken more than a few seconds."

Leaving nothing more than a blurred half-footprint and a few minor stains after such a bloody murder was something of an art, Embla thought. And she still found it weird that he hadn't at least taken the silver goblet with him. Him . . . ?

"Could the killer have been a woman?" she burst out before she'd had time to think it through.

Her boss raised an eyebrow. "Shoe size forty-one—I shouldn't think so," he said, clearly amused.

Before the laughter spread too far among the team, Irene Huss slammed a boot-clad foot on the table. "Size forty-one," she informed them.

Laughter quickly turned to a bout of coughing and throat-clearing. Irene was six feet tall, so it was hardly surprising that she had big feet. Embla gave her a grateful look. Because Embla was the youngest member of the department, Tommy had a tendency to pat her on the head, or give her a hard time. He did it with a smile and under the guise of banter, but Embla knew exactly what he was doing: master suppression techniques. *Bastard!* she thought.

With her foot still resting on the table, Irene went on: "If it does turn out to be a woman, then we should be looking at the old lady."

This time Tommy couldn't help laughing out loud. "Seriously? An eighty-nine-year-old who's nearly deaf and suffering from early stages of dementia? You're suggesting she killed a man who was half her age and twice her size? Then she climbed out of the window and down the scaffolding to the sidewalk? I don't think so. She uses a *wheeled walker*, for God's sake!"

The others didn't hesitate to join in with the laughter this time. Only Irene and Embla remained serious.

. If you allow yourself to entertain the thought . . . then suddenly it makes sense.

She might have found him stealing the silver after she let him in herself. But . . . she slept in the apartment for several nights with the dead body in her father's room. And she really did seem terribly upset and confused when we arrived that Saturday morning after she'd found him. Eighty-nine . . . No, it's not possible. Then again . . .

As time went by and the investigation remained at a standstill, Embla's thoughts would run along the same lines many times.

A FEW DAYS before Christmas, Tommy Persson informed the team, "We're shelving the Frazzén homicide. The new cases that have come in over the past few weeks are piling up, and that's where we need to target our resources."

Congratulations, little Maud. You got away with it, Embla said to herself with an ironic smile.

(2018)

H ELENE TURSTEN WAS a nurse and a dentist before she turned to writing. She is the author of two mystery series set in Gothenburg, Sweden: the Irene Huss investigations (*Detective Inspector Huss*, *Night Rounds*, *The Torso*, *The Glass Devil*, *The Golden Calf*, *The Fire Dance*, *The Beige Man*, *The Treacherous Net*, *Who Watcheth*, and *Protected by the Shadows*) and the Embla Nyström investigations, beginning with *Hunting Game*.

After spending years writing about honest people who work hard to uphold the law, Helene was inspired to write about someone on the *other* side of the law:

> "*One of the biggest publishers in Sweden asked me for a story for their Christmas anthology. I said yes, but then I realized that I didn't know what story to tell. The deadline came closer, and I felt totally*

empty. I almost panicked. And then she came to me: Maud. She was 88 years old and looked like most old grannies. But inside she was quite special. Her age was a perfect disguise for a criminal! Even . . . a murderer. I wrote the first story, "An Elderly Lady Seeks Peace at Christmastime," in just three hours, and I enjoyed every minute of her company. But let's just say I would not like to have her for a neighbor or a relative!"

Thus, the collection of stories featuring the irascible Maud, *An Elderly Lady Is Up to No Good*, was born.

Helene's books have been translated into twenty-one languages and made into a Swedish television series. She was born in Gothenburg, where she now lives with her husband, and the couple has one daughter.

empty. I almost panicked. And then she came to me: Maud. She was 88 years old and looked like most old grannies. But inside she was quite special. Her age was a perfect disguise for a criminal! Even . . . a murderer. I wrote the first story, "An Elderly Lady Seeks Peace at Christmastime," in just three hours, and I enjoyed every minute of her company. But let's just say I would not like to have her for a neighbor or a relative!"

Thus, the collection of stories featuring the irascible Maud, *An Elderly Lady Is Up to No Good*, was born.

Helene's books have been translated into twenty-one languages and made into a Swedish television series. She was born in Gothenburg, where she now lives with her husband, and the couple has one daughter.